SONNY LISTON'S EYES
& COLLECTED PLAYS

KEITH G. LAUFENBERG

SONNY LISTON'S EYES & COLLECTED PLAYS

KEITH G. LAUFENBERG

PUBLISHED BY ROYAL CROWN ROYAL, LLC

Florida
Printed in the United States of America
ISBN 13: 978-1-944699-04-8 (Plays)
ISBN 13: 978-1-944699-05-5 (e-book)

Royal Crown Royal Publishing

Copyright © 2016 by Keith G. Laufenberg

All rights reserved. No part of these Plays (book) may be reproduced, stored in a retrieval system or transmitted in any form, except as a play, on stage, with the permission of the author, or by any means without the prior written permission of the publishers, except by a reviewer who may quote passages in a review to be printed in a newspaper, magazine or journal.

FIRST EDITION

For *God*, the *Father*, the creator of all things and everything eternal, and for those human beings who love the truth, something I search for constantly, especially whenever I sit down at my computer and remember and, sometimes, even imagine.

And for my family, my wife of 41 years, Andrea and my four children, Amanda, Natalie, Danny and Denise, who have made my life a happier, easier journey and also, my five grandchildren, Michael and Noelle, Avery and McKinley and Devon whose names always bring a smile to my face.

The following plays have been previously published, as stories: "Sonny Liston's Eyes" in *The Spillway Review*, 2006; *Author Trek*, 2007 and *The Manly Art in* 2014; "Bad Medicine" in *OMG Magazine, 2008;* "Big Sugar" in *Short Story.Me*, 2010; *Muhammad's Revenge*, 2014; "My Name is Nobody" in *Mobius Magazine*, 2011 & *Any Other Name,* 2014; "Mr. Payback" in *Streetlife*, 2014; "The Gun" in *First Step Press*, 1998 and in *Streetlife*, 2014.

BOOKS BY KEITH G. LAUFENBERG

<u>Available in bookstores & e-stores worldwide</u>

NOVELS

MIAMI ROCK
SEMPER-FI-DO-OR-DIE
THE TOWER OF POWER
THE PROFIT FACTOR
SOUTH OF SOUTH BEACH
THE ANXIOUS ASSASSINS

SHORT STORY COLLECTIONS

MUHAMMAD'S REVENGE
STREETLIFE
BADMEDICINE
COWBOYS & INDIANS
THE MANLY ART
SAVING PRIMO
ANY OTHER NAME

POETRY CHAPBOOK

I AM AN AMERICAN

PLAYS

LIBERTY CITY-THE PLAY
SONNY LISTON'S EYES & COLLECTED PLAYS
PEACE ON EARTH & COLLECTED PLAYS
SANTA CLAUS, SATELLITES, CELLPHONES & SINKHOLES, IN SPRING HILL & COLLECTED PLAYS

CONTENTS

-1- SONNY LISTON'S EYES …......6
-2- BAD MEDICINE …..................45
-3- BIG SUGAR …........................62
-4- THE SHEIK IS DEAD ….........89
-5- My NAME IS NOBODY …....132
-6- MR. PAYBACK …................142
-7- THE GUN ….........................155

For All Plays Herein: (*Beat*) A *Beat* is a pause of unspecified length but usually very short.
(*Pause*) Length is determined and set by an agreement between the writer, director and actor(s).

SONNY LISTON'S EYES

AN ORIGINAL PLAY IN THREE ACTS

CHARACTERS:

GARY GREB: WRITER, AGE 53
JACKIE McGUIRE: FRIEND OF GREB, AGE 53
ANTHONY ROMANICO; AKA TONY ROME: AGE 70+

ACT I

A TELEPHONE CONVERSATION BETWEEN GARY GREB, WHO IS IN ATLANTA AND HIS FRIEND JACKIE BYRNE, IN NEW YORK, AND THEN A SUBSEQUENT CONVERSATION BETWEEN GREB AND TONY ROME CONVINCES GREB THAT HE SHOULD ACCEPT A ROUND-TRIP TICKET TO NEW YORK TO SEE IF WHAT TONY ROME CLAIMS AS TRUTH HAS ENOUGH MERIT TO REQUIRE AN INTERVIEW AND SUBSEQUENT BOOK.

ACT I SCENES & SETTINGS

2 Scenes: Setting is telephone conversations between the 3 characters Gary Greb, who is in Atlanta and Jackie Byrne and Anthony Romanico both in New York.

ACT II

GREB MEETS WITH TONY ROME AND BECOMES PRIVY TO AN UNBELIEVABLE AND ALMOST INCOMPREHENSIBLE STORY ABOUT THE MAFIA AND THEIR CONTRACTS AND DEALINGS IN SUCH THINGS AS ASSASSINATIONS WITH THE AMERICAN GOVERNMENT AND OTHER FOREIGN GOVERNMENTS AND JUST HOPES HE CAN RETRIEVE HIS TAPE RECORDER FROM HIS FRIEND'S HOUSE BEFORE IT'S TOO LATE.

ACT II SCENES & SETTINGS

2 Scenes: Both settings are in New York. Scene 1 is in Jackie Byrne's house; scene 2 is in Anthony Romanico's house.

INTERMISSION

ACT III

GREB HAS THE STORY, NOW ALL HE NEEDS IS TO GET HIS TAPE RECORDER AT HIS FRIEND'S HOUSE TO GET THE WHOLE THING ON TAPE BEFORE IT'S TOO LATE.

ACT III   SCENES & SETTINGS

2 Scenes: Next day; Jackie Byrne's kitchen. Tony Rome's house.

ACT I
SCENE 1

Setting: Phone conversation between Gary Greb and Jackie Byrne. Greb is in his home in Atlanta and Byrne is in his home, in Howard Beach, Queens, New York on January 4, 2000.

GARY GREB: Hey Bodiddley, wah'sup? (*No recognizable accent but with some dialectic words*)
JACKIE BYRNE: G-Man, there's a guy up here youse should talk to, he's a hit-man for the mob. Claims he clipped everybody from J.F.K. to Sonny Liston. And, I tol' him youse knew Liston, youse boxed wid 'im didn't yah? (*Heavy New York accent combined with many dialectic words*)
(*Beat.*)
GARY GREB: What's the deal anyway? Yah shittin' me, Jack-oh?
(*Beat*)
JACKIE BYRNE: Naw I wouldn't shit yah Jamie, youse ah my favorite turd. Heh, anyway, this guy just lives right up the street from me man, t'ree houses away. Says he's ready to tell his story; yeah, and youse can be the writer of his autobiography. Bumped off all these guys? King too. Yah livin' down there in Atlanta youse oughta be interested in that one?
(*Beat.*)
GARY GREB: King? You mean Martin Luther King Junior?
(*Beat*)
JACKIE BYRNE: Yeah, he was the shooter. This is yah big break man, y'know?
GARY GREB: If it's that big a story why get a nickel-and-dime writer like me? Why'nt he get some big shot right there in New York, like

Norman Mailer or Mario Puzo or some other hot-shot like 'at?
(*Pause*)
JACKIE BYRNE: He read some of yah short stories, in 'ose magazines youse sent me man, and he really liked 'em man. He thinks yah a good writer and yah the best man for the job, says he can see youse write the truth and will know it when yah hear it.
(*Beat*)
GARY GREB: (*smiling because of the writing compliments.*) Sounds like you're feeding me a line Johnny?
JACKIE BYRNE: No way man. Look, this guy was a hit-man for the mob; hey there's a good title G-man. Hit man for the mob admits to, yah know, all these hits, what ah youse t'ink?
GARY GREB: Jackie, I'm here in Atlanta and you guys are in New York?
(*Beat*)
JACKIE BYRNE: He'll send yah plane fare man. What ah youse t'ink about that? Dude's real man.
(*Beat*)
GARY GREB: I dunno man I just started another day-job?
JACKIE BYRNE: What, sellin' cars again, G-man?
GARY GREB: Naw, man, mortgages. Plus a scumbag my wife knows is givin' me some side work. (*Scumbag was the code-name they had for lawyers.*)
JACKIE BYRNE: Side woik for a scumbag huh, what ah youse doin', resoich?"
(*Beat*)
GARY GREB: Research shit, I'm investigatin' a guy. Workin' for a criminal lawyer but, I guess I *could* put it off for a few days; but man, I dunno Jocko? I just gave her a bill for seven bucks and she paid me like it was nothin'. Did about four hours work, y'know?
JACKIE BYRNE: Yeah, seven hundred huh? Some ah dem female lawyahs ain't too swift, huh?
(*Beat*)

GARY GREB: She's got plenty smarts upstairs Jamie, the people she's got are payin' her big green. This con-man wants to marry their daughter. I ran his bureau, checked up on his record and the dude's a two-time loser; a real flim-flam man.
JACKIE BYRNE: No shit. Look G-Man, you comin' up or not? I can always call Woodward and Bernstein, yah know?
(*Beat*)
GARY GREB: (*laughs*) Jackie, okay, say this guy wants me to write his autobiography and he really assassinated these guys? The mob would kill him? Why would he …?
(*Beat*)
BYRNE: The mob ain't got nothin' on his lung cancer G-Man, he's had sixty days to live for the last six months now and says he knows he's on his last legs, or oxygen tanks in this case. I tell you what man; I'll have him call youse, how 'bout that?
(*Beat*)
GREB: No shit he's dyin'?
BYRNE: Yup, any day now, wait'll yah see 'im in poisun? Look, just keep an open mind and listen to 'im; should I tell 'im to call youse?
(*Pause*)
GREB: Sure, why not; tell 'im to call me man, what the hell, can't hurt.
(*Beat*)
BYRNE: Ten-four Johnny. Semper-Fi. (*Both men had served in the Marines.*)
GREB: Ten-four Jackie, Semper-Fi.

SCENE 2

Setting: Greb is sitting by a phone in his house.

GREB: (*Two hours have passed when the phone rings.*) Hello?

(*Beat*)
TONY ROME: Hey, diz Tony Rome, youse a frien' ah Jackie Boine, cah-peesh?
(*Beat*)
GREB: (*Sees, on his caller I.D. the name Anthony Romanico.*) Yeah, so you're Tony Rome huh?
ROME: Dat's me man, cah-peesh?
(*Beat*)
GREB: Yeah, Jackie said something about you bumped off a lotta famous people?
(*Beat*)
ROME: Yeah, ahawhooo-heeee-aaaccccck, ahhwhooooweee …
(*Pause*)
GREB: (*Listens to sixty seconds of hacking and coughing and heavy breathing and wonders if he truly is within days of death.*) Hey man, are you alright? Hey are you …
(*Beat*)
ROME: Yeah … ahah … ah yeah. My lungs man, don't ever start smokin' youse know? I hear youse was a boxer in Vegas, cah-peesh?
(*Beat*)
GREB: Yeah, I was for about a year, turned pro there and fought in Dee Cee and Miami Beach and L-lay, later on in my life.
(*Beat*)
ROME: Hey, sounds like yousah got aroun' huh? I used tah box a lil' myself cah-peesh?
(*Pause*)
GREB: So you're gonna tell me the whole story huh?
(*Beat*)
ROME: That's the deal man. I read those stories youse have published in several of dose magazines and I like dem, cah-peesh? Youse gonna get my story exclew-sine, cah-peesh?
(*Pause*)
GREB: (*Realizing his buddy Jackie was not beyond a practical joke,*

Greb also realizes all he knew about this guy was his voice and incessant hacking and that he ended most of his sentences with capisci, which he knew was Italian for understand. He knew a bit about Sonny Liston and decided to test Tony Rome.) Say ah, you say you clipped Sonny Liston, right?

(*Pause*)

ROME: Sonny, yeah, ah, dat eggplant was a scary bastid. I had help on 'at one dough, cah-peesh?

(*Beat*)

GREB: Yeah, you had help with that melanzane, with that jah-mook, huh?

(*Pause*)

ROME: (*Laughs and coughs*) Ah, I see youse speak a lil' Italian, a paisan?

GREB: Yeah, very little, what kinna help did you have with Sonny?

(*Beat*)

ROME: I had a broad put some dust in 'is drink. One t'ing I'll never forget about Sonny though, I can tell yah dat, cah-peesh?

GREB: Yeah, what's that?

ROME: His eyes; Sonny had some cold, hard eyes, right up to the end too, cah-peesh?

(*Beat*)

GREB: Tony, you gonna pick up my freight for a round-trip airfare right?

(*Beat*)

ROME: Dat's what I told Jackie; sure I will, cah-peesh?

(*Beat*)

GREB: Cah-peesh Tony; I'll see you soon. (*The next plane, leaving from Atlanta to New York, left at 3:00 a.m., the next morning and Gary Greb, who had known Sonny Liston's ways, both from what he had heard from other fighters and what he had personally observed, was on it.*)

ACT II
SCENE 1

Setting: Jackie Byrne's house. Greb has slept on the plane and at Jackie's house. It is now just past noon.

BYRNE: (*Sitting at kitchen table*) Yeah, G-Man, diz video store overcharged me on late fees; their computer registered that I owed them for an entire century.
(*Beat*)
GREB: Y-two-kay, huh Jackie?
BYRNE: Yeah, said I owed 'em ninety large man.
GREB: Yeah, bullshit huh? Gonna bring scam-artists by the thousands outta the woodwork, man? Man, I'm still beat. Hey what's with this Tony Rome dude anyway? What's his real name? My caller eye-dee read Anthony Romanico?
BYRNE: Yeah, that's it; he claims another nickname besides Tony Rome too.
(*Beat*)
GREB: Yeah, another street-name? What?
BYRNE: Dead-Eye. And, guess how he got the name Dead-Eye G-man?
(*Beat*)
GREB: How would I know? I only talked to him long enough to realize he knew enough about Liston to have known him and, shee-it, I guess he knew enough about his ways to get him at the right time, so it looked like a suicide.
BYRNE: Sure he did G-Man. I'm tellin' youse he popped him; that's right Jamie, he clipped 'im. Got 'is name in 'Nam too. That's right brother, he was in 'Nam. There was this sniper all us Mow-reenes had nicknamed Dead-Eye, an NVA sniper, and Tony Rome popped *him*.

(Beat)
GREB: And he wants to tell his story to me because he read some of my short stories; like Frankenstein and Liberty City?
BYRNE: Yup and The Terror too. Hates Russia and Russians. He offed a bunch of 'em over in Sheepshead Bay.
(Beat)
GREB: Sounds like a real *nice* guy?
(Beat)
BYRNE: (*Laughs*)Yeah, well, he's dyin' soon, you'll see that real quick G-Man, but, then, who knows? Dude came out of an oxygen tent. Youse din' hear him hackin' and coughin' on ah phone.
(Beat)
GREB: I heard it man.
BYRNE: Wait'll youse see what he's got in his house, you'll be a believer then.
GREB: Yeah, what's he got, a couple ah bodies in 'is refrigerator?
BYRNE: (*Laughs*) Jus' wait G-Man, you'll believe him; mark my woids Jake, mark my woids.
(Beat.)
GREB: Mark your words? Heh-heh. Consider 'em marked then Jack-oh.
(*Light fades away*)

SCENE 2

Setting: As the light comes up we see Tony Rome's mailbox and then the front door, which enters onto center stage from the front door, stage left.

BYRNE: There's his house. (*Tony Rome is stenciled, in big, black letters, on his mailbox and it takes almost a solid minute of ringing his doorbell before he answers the door.*) Hey Tony, what's up?

(*Pause*)
TONY ROME: (*coughs and hacks out a greeting*) Hey, Jackie, and diz is dah writah, I guess, cah-peesh?
BYRNE: Yeah, yeah Tony diz is Gary Greb, the G-Man.
(*Pause*)
ROME: (*Sticks his hand out towards Greb, who shakes hands with him.*) Hah-heh-heh, ahwhooowhee aaack; the G-Man, hah-hah. C'mon in, I gotta bottle ah vino in ah kitchen. Gee-zuz, I'd give my life fer a cigarette. I'm down to one a day and I had it diz mawnin' ahhooo...eeeaccck. Funny t'ing it's dah only t'ing 'at stops me from coughin' like diz … ahhhahwhooeeeaack. Ain't dat a bitch? Ah whoowheee accckk.
GREB: (*Glances at Jackie and they both smile. Tony Rome is holding a portable oxygen tank in his left hand and two oxygen hoses were rammed into his nostrils: he didn't look like he could take too much vino.*) Nice kitchen Tony.
(*Beat*)
ROME: (*Removes tubes from his nose.*) Youse guys join me in a drink, cah-peesh. (*Pours three glasses about half-full then holds his glass out towards Byrne and Greb.*) Sah-lood, sah-lood, Alla too-ah sah-lood!
(*Pause*)
BYRNE: (*Touches his glass against Tony Rome's and then Greb's.*) Salute.
GREB: Salute.
ROME: (*Takes a long swallow of wine and eyeballs Greb.*) Youse gonna write it the way I tell youse to, cah-peesh?
(*Pause*)
GREB: Sure man, why wouldn't I? (*Looks at Jackie Byrne and shakes his head.*)
(*Pause*)
BYRNE: Hey Tony, how about showin' the G-Man here yah trophy room?
(*Beat*)

GREB: Trophy room …? (*Remembers that Jackie had promised that he'd be a believer when he saw the inside of Tony Rome's house and he and Byrne exchange glances*)

(*Pause*)

ROME: Yeah, I can see youse need sumpin' to convince youse dat I am who I say I am. C'mon, follow me, den, cah-peesh? (*Leads them into another room, where, inside, are numerous weapons, pistols and rifles, bayonets and dead hand-grenade casings, along with uniforms and insignias from the Vietnam War. There were also numerous pictures with Tony Rome in his Marine Corps uniform, at different duty stations around the globe.*)

BYRNE: (*nods towards a rifle with a ventilated barrel and folding stock*) That's a Swedish K. Only dudes had those in 'Nam was the spooks.

(*Beat*)

ROME: Yeah dat's right, youse right Jackie, we uz the only outfit 'at had 'em.

(*Pause*)

GREB: What? *You* were a spook? You were with the CIA?

ROME: Sorta. I'm like an honorary membah, cah-peesh?

(*Beat*)

GREB: What? Wha' … why … I mean …?

ROME: I was sent over to the 'Nam when I was only 19 youse know but I could already shoot like nobody youse ever saw, or the Mow-reenes eithah. Why, I could shoot the eyes outta a snipah at five-hundred yards.

(*Beat*)

GREB: Bu' … but you grew up in New York, where …?

ROME: I had a lil' pistol, a twenty-two caliber, when I was seven and a .30-30 rifle when I was ten, and my daddy took me to the range every week, cah-peesh?

BYRNE: His dad was a cop G-Man.

(*Beat*)

ROME: *(Nods at Greb.)* Yeah, poor suckah got shot in dah line ah duty when he was toy-tee-nine. (*Hands a picture to Greb*) This was taken in Jay-Vil' in fitty-seben.

GREB: *(Takes picture from Rome and looks at it.)* You was in the Air Wing? I was too; got my training at Jacksonville in sixty-two. That's what? About five years apart, huh?

ROME: Yup, I got trained as a sixty-four twelve, cah-peesh?

GREB: Man, that's a jet mechanic, ain't it?

ROME: Yeah, but when they found out I shot two-fifty they trained me for sniper duty, cah-peesh?

(*Beat*.)

GREB: Two-fifty, man, that's 100% bulls-eyes**,** as good as you can get? *Nobody* shoots two-fifty?

(*Beat*)

ROME: Nobody but me, cah-peesh. (*Rome hands Greb another picture*.) That's in Atsugi in Jay-pan. Dah Marine Air Control Squad I was in for awhile, in late fifty-seven, early fifty-eight, cah-peesh?

(*Beat*).

GREB: (*Looks at picture*.) What's this got to do with anything?

(*Pause*)

ROME: (*Eyeballs Jackie Byrne, who then motions to Greb with his hands to be patient. Greb takes another picture that Rome now hands him.*) Jus' wait a minute, cah-peesh? See that's in El Toro, in fifty-eight. See that guy I'm standin' next to in both pich-urs?

(*Beat*)

GREB: (*Looks at pictures again*) Yeah-yeah, I see that … who …

(*Beat*)

ROME: Yeah, he got out a year later but we still kept in touch; he even wrote me when I was in 'Nam, right up until I got out in sixty-two and me and him we wuz close Pally, real close.

GREB: (*Looks at Byrne and then Rome and puts his hands, palms up, out and shakes his head.*) What's that go to do …

(*Pause.*)

ROME: Take a closer look at the other Marine in 'ose pictures and tell me youse nevah seen dat face before, *writer,* cah-peesh?
(*Beat.*)
GREB: (*Looking at pictures. Looks startled and exhales a long breath of air.*) Sssshhh, that's Oswald, ain't it?
(*Beat.*)
ROME: (*Looks at Byrne and they both laugh.*) Took yah long enough.
(*Pause*)
BYRNE: Yeah, youse gettin' the picture now, huh? (his smile widens) I tol' youse G-Man.
GREB: Man, how, I mean how did you ever get to … you know to …
ROME: I was already wid ah eye by then and mobbed up. I was back maybe t'ree months when I got a chance to get my button, cah-peesh?
(*Beat.*)
GREB: Your button?
ROME: Yeah, din' youse see the Godfaddah, ahahaheerah…ahhhacck ..
(*Long Pause: coughing fit.*)
GREB: Man Jackie, dude's in terrible shape. (*Rome is desperately grabbing the oxygen tank on the table and shoves the tubes up his nostrils. After maybe five minutes he gets his breath back.*)
(*Pause*)
ROME: Yeah, I had a chance to get made just like 'at and 'at ain't often. They had ah books open in sixty-t'ree and see, they wanted Kennedy dusted off so I took the contract.
(*Pause*)
GREB: (*Looks dumbfounded at the audience*) Who … the mob …?
(*Beat.*)
ROME: Them and the Eye.
(*Pause*)
GREB: The CIA and the mob were workin' together?
(*Beat.*)
ROME: They did it all ah the time pally, still do.
(*Pause*)

GREB: (*Looks dumbfound at audience and shakes head*) Yeah, so but, how did you …

ROME: I was still in touch with Lee at this time and when we found out he had tried to clip Walker but missed and he was woikin' at the depository in Dallas, well we …

GREB: Wait a minute—he tried to clip Walker? Who's Walker?

ROME: A retired army general who was livin' in Dallas and who was into politics that Lee didn't agree wid; but Lee didn't agree wid hardly anybody's politics. Anyway, he tried to shoot the guy. He couldn't even hit him from a hundred yards. One t'ing I can tell youse fah sure; Lee could-din shoot: any t'ing he hit was an accident, cah-peesh?
(*Beat*)

GREB: (*Looks at audience, dumbfounded, yet again*) Well then how did he get the …

ROME: … I jus' tol' youse, he didn't, I did. Once we knew he was woikin' at the depository we made sure it was onna route Kennedy was takin' and then we talked him into helpin' us. See, Lee was a commie, he was a little nuts yah know but like I said, he was no shooter, cah-peesh?
(*Beat*)

GREB: Yeah, well I went You-n-que myself but then I never was a shooter either. But two-fifty, hell that's a bull's eye every fuggin' time. I never heard ah anybody shootin' two-fifty on ah range, like I said Tony, I mean it defies logic. Two-fifty? (*Looks at audience, shrugs his shoulders and puts palms upwards to show just how unbelievable it is to him.*)
(*Beat*)

ROME: Why youse t'ink they call me Dead-Eye; I offed a Vee-Cee snipah that t'ought he was me, hehah. Yeah Lee never was a shooter eithah, hell he barely made sharpshooter and that's onna stationary target, c'mon, I hadda pop Kennedy while he was in a moving car and from more than five hundred yards. Lee was set-up; he just didn't realize it 'till they arrested him. Tippet was just icing onna cake for us, cah-peesh G-Man? Ah-heh-haa, G-Man, youse shouldah been wid us, hah-heh, G-Man, like dat sissy J. Edgar, hated sissies 'cause he was one.

Yeah, anyway, like I say Tippet, he was real icing on dah cake.
(*Beat*.)
GREB: Tippet …?
ROME: Yeah, Tippet. He'us dah cop Lee shot after he took off from the depository. See, we had a poifect shot at Kennedy; we wuz up in a position over onna grassy knoll area, yeah we had a Ford pick-up truck and we had a hole in ah tailgate where I stuck the rifle, a freakin' antique but I used it, and a sheet ah plywood coverin' the top and as soon as Lee opened up I put one right into JFK's t'roat and another in 'is skull; man we wuz gone before anybody knew we wuz even there, and Lee's instructions were to get rid of *his* weapon and beat it outta town. The only t'ing I din' like was usin' dat six-point-five bolt action Carcano but den I practiced wid it on ah range for two weeks straight before I made the shot; just shows yah only one Deadeye and 'at's me. We even had some spooks and mob guys shootin' too and also dey was dere in case anybody seen the truck pull away but nobody did. Lee, he t'ought he mighta hit Kennedy, a real eggplant he was and it woiked out real good for us, cah-peesh dere Gary?
(*Pause*)
GREB: Wait! Wait a minute. The CIA and the mob both were there shooting at, **AT JFK?**
ROME: Dey was always dere on most ah my hits, youse kiddin' me?
(*Pause*)
GREB: And Oswald knew about 'em? (*Looks at audience as if he's getting too much unbelievable information at one time and throws his hands up in the air*)
(*Beat*)
ROME: Lee knew about it sure; he was woikin' fah both ah 'em but Lee was nevah altogether there, cah-peesh? He was crazy; really crazy but then who wasn't? I know I was, cah-peesh G-Man?
(*Beat*)
GREB: What about Jack Ruby? I mean if …
ROME: (*Cuts Greb off in mid-sentence.*) … Ruby was wid us, cah-

peesh G-Man?

(*Beat.*)

GREB: Look, I dunno about Oswald or Ruby but I did know Sonny Liston and …

ROME: (*Continues to cut Greb off and hands him a pair of bronzed boxing gloves.*) These were Sonny's; the ones he kayoed Patterson wid. I took 'em outta his house, cah-peesh G-Man?

GREB: Tony, you killed him then took *evidence* from his house? Where'd he live?

(*Beat*)

ROME: It didn't mattah if I took sumpin' from 'is house, nobody cared about Sonny, they barely investigated it; the local cops were all onna pad. Sonny had a nice place, his backyard overlooked the sixteenth green of the Stardust Country Club, right on ah golf-course. Got it from Kirk Kerkorian, a wheeler-dealer who owns more real estate than Donald Trump, in Vegas anyways, lived on Ottawa Drive and about a mile from his pal Joe Louis, who was on smack and kept buggin' Sonny that he hadda pay too much for it. So, Sonny gets some from the wiseguys and they give it up for nuttin', figurin' it's for Joe but Sonny has these other punks wantin' his help too, so he gets more sayin' it's for Joe an then he sells it to these addicts and pockets the difference, cah-peesh G-Man?

(Pause.)

GREB: And they killed him for that? I remember the papers sayin' he overdosed on heroin? Look, Tony, I knew a lotta fighters 'at knew Sonny better'n me and he had a psycho aversion to needles. And yet, they found him dead of an overdose with the needle still in his arm? (*Looks at audience like he's right and Rome must be lying.*)

ROME: Awheeaack, wait, cah-peesh G-Man? (*Tony Rome struggled for breath, and ran to get his oxygen tank, again.*)

(*Pause*)

BYRNE: What'd I tell youse G-Man? Guy's real. What ayah t'ink?

(*Beat.*)

GREB: If half of what he says is true, it'll be like hitting the lottery. Man, I know of at least a half-dozen publishing houses and newspapers that would pay through the nose for a story like this. Not that Sonny Liston 'ill be the story; no, the story's gonna be JFK and Martin Luther King, Jr. but I don't know nothin' about those guys personally. But, Sonny Liston I know a little bit about and know a lotta guys who knew him too and when I was there observing him in the gym and talkin' to the guy and then in '72 when I was passin' through Vegas and stopped to fight 'cause my car broke down there I ...
BYRNE: Yeah, when you fought on a couple day's ah trainin' huh G-Man?
GREB: Yeah, barely a week and every fighter there that I talked to said the mob killed Sonny too.
(*Beat*)
BYRNE: Tony Rome ain't lyin' G-Man?
GREB: I'm startin' to believe him too.
(*Pause.*)
ROME: (*Comes back with his oxygen tank and a watch in his hand. It was bejeweled and expensive-looking, with a thin golden band. A woman's watch, obviously. He handed it to Greb.*) Look on ah back ah it, cah-peesh Gary?
(*Beat*)
GREB: (*Greb turns the watch over and on the gold band, just under '24k', it read: 'To Mary, Love Sonny.' Jackie Byrne comes over and glances at it also.*) C'mon, Tony, this don't mean nothin' to me. Anybody could ah done that inscription?
ROME: Yeah but they didn't. I got it from diz broad Mary. She was a low-life but Sonny was sweet on her, cah-peesh? He knew her when she was a real high-class hooker; hundred an hour she got. Used to call her Mary the mouth 'cause she could get youse excited jus' by lickin' her lips, yah know wha' I mean? The booze did her in finally but she was still lookin' good in 1970, when she helped me wid Sonny. She died a couple ah years after Sonny ah cee-rosis ah dah livah, called her Vodka-

job Mary at the end, 'cause she'd blow a guy for a glass ah vodka. Yeah, ain't life funny dough?

GREB: Tony, I remember a broad like that, used to work at the Dee-Eye and the Sahara named Mary. This broad looked a lot like Dolly Parton and she …

ROME: (*Cuts Greb off.*) … Yeah, dat was dah broad, aw'right, she used tah be a high-priced piece ah moy-chindice I kin tell youse dat fer sure, cah-peesh G-Man?

GREB: Tony, if this is the same broad I remember then I remember she liked fighters, some kind of a strange passion for boxers, we always saw her at the fights at the Silver Slipper and the Castaways and I remember her at a title fight at the Convention Center between Jose Torres and Eddie Cotton.

(*Beat*)

ROME: Jackie tells me youse fought out dere huh? I remember a kid called Kayo, was that youse, cah-peesh?

(*Beat*.)

GREB: (*Smiles and pounds his chest towards the audience*) I see you know more about me than you're lettin' on, huh?

ROME: Naw-aww, I remember youse now Kayo. Youse fought a southpaw at the Slipper once when I was there. I remember youse lost a split decision.

(*Beat*)

GREB: Only southpaw I fought in Vegas was Wade Smith and I lost a decision alright. Dude named Andy Kendall was working my corner and had me fightin' too aggressively, I'm a natural counter-puncher and so was Wade Smith. He was also a pretty good fighter man. How you know me as Kayo? I mean, I did have it on my robe but there was only one guy really who called me that.

(*Beat*)

ROME: Ralph told me 'bout youse, said he'us gonna take youse wid 'im when he went back to Austree-dah."

GREB: You knew Dupas? He never did get back there man. And it was

Australia not Austria.

ROME: Yeah, he was woikin at the D-Eye fer awhile as a doorman, youse know? Former world champ and all but after Joe Louis did it, youse know all the ex-champs did that, cah-peesh G-Man?

(*Beat.*)

GREB: Yeah but, let's face it Tony, Joe was all drugged out.

(*Beat.*)

ROME: So was Sonny by dat time, but he got drunk on J-un-B instead ah *Horse*, cah-peesh G-Man?

(*Pause*)

GREB: So, Tony, this Mary helped you clip Liston?

ROME: Yeah, she put some dust in 'is Scotch, just before I popped a needle into his veins, cah-peesh G-Man?

(*Beat*)

GREB: A needle, huh? Heroin huh? C'mon Tony Sonny'd never …

ROME: (*interrupts Greb.*) Yeah, I know what youse ah t'inkin', cah-peesh? Sonny was afraid ah needles and he din' do drugs and that's all true, but, like I said, nobody gave a shit about Sonny. And, the heroin was a good, extra touch 'cause, like youse now know, his idol, Joe Louis was on dah *Horse,* cah-peesh Gary?

GREB: That was in the papers Tony or should I say Dead-Eye?

(*Beat*)

ROME: Either one; Anthony Romanico is my real name, cah-peesh G-Man?

GREB: Tony Rome's your street name then?

ROME: Yeah but youse never hoid ah me, cah-peesh G-Man?

(*Beat*)

GREB: How do you know? Fighter's in Vegas knew a lot of mob guys Tony?

ROME: Yeah, but not me Pally. Not me G- Man.

GREB: No? You were too big then, huh? But we knew all the low-life's Tony, they liked to hang around the gym and the fights, you know?

(*Beat*)

ROME: Sure, I know Pally and I went to the fights a lot too, like I said, but nobody knew I was dere, 'cept me Pally, cahpeesh G-Man?

GREB: I still don't get why you guys had to kill Sonny, I mean it wasn't like he …

ROME: (interrupts) … I tell you why, he knew too much Pally, cahpeesh? He threatened to spill his guts once too often for us because he hadda big mouth when he was on that Jay and Bee Scotch, cah-peesh?

GREB: Yeah but what in ah hell could he tell anybody, c'mon Tony he was washed up by then. That dude from Phillie knocked him out in sixty-nine, Leotis Martin, and he used to be Sonny's sparring partner. Anyway, Sonny was way over the hill in nineteen-seventy.

ROME: Sonny t'rew both fights to Clay, cah-peesh Gary? (*Beat*.)

GREB: C'mon man, no way, no way. Ali was too much for Sonny, too fast, took too good a punch and he psyched Sonny out.

(*Beat*)

ROME: Know what Pally. He may have been all dat but he din' get a *real* chance to prove it. Youse got any idea how much we made on 'ose fights? Sonny was a nine to five favorite in the second fight until Clay had the hernia and the odds started changin' to even money. We got seven to one if Sonny tanked in ah fois'; which, as you know, he did. Hell, the boys in Cleveland got over t'ree mil-yun just themselves. C'mon man, Sonny was a scary bastid but he did what he was told when Frankie tol' 'im to.

GREB: Frankie?

ROME: Yeah, Frankie Carbo, cah-peesh G-Man?

GREB: What? Man, c'mon I seen Liston get up before the count of ten, if it hadn't ah been for that idiot referee, Jersey Joe Walcott; how could a guy be such a good fighter himself and then blow the count like that?

ROME: It wasn't Jersey Joe; it was Nat Fly-sha that told Jersey Joe to stop it, cah-peesh G-Man?

(*Pause*)

GREB: (*Mouth agape, obviously doesn't believe this statement. Walks*

towards the audience and throws hands up in the air) Wha …ah …uht? Nat Fleisher? You had the publisher of Ring Magazine onnah pad?
ROME: Let's jus' say we got our ways ah protectin' our money. Look, Sonny knew he was supposed to tank and when he got hit and went down he was supposed to stay down but he always had too much pride and he got up. We had to have insurance. We had a lotta money on 'at fight, cah-peesh Gary? Like I just said everybody got well on it and the fois' fight was even bettah, we got eight to one in 'at fight, made a killin' Pally, a real killin' and Sonny got paid in at fois' fight too, cah-peesh Gary?
(Beat)
GREB: C'mon Tony, if that's true how come they couldn't prove it? I mean the F.B.I. would have known if there were a big payoff on the fight, wouldn't they?
ROME: The Eye knew, the spooks knew too, they all knew, cah-peesh? Dey was all in on it, cah-peesh G-Man?
(Pause)
GREB: C'mon Tony. The FBI and the CIA were both in on those assassinations? *(Looks at audience and throws up hands.)*
(Pause)
ROME: Yeh, dey was Gary, dey was, cah-peesh?
(Pause)
GREB: Yeah, but that first fight man, I mean, he quit in the corner?
ROME: Sonny hated Clay so much he wanted to kill him: so we gave 'im six rounds, cah-peesh Gary?
(Pause)
GREB: *(Looks at Tony as if he's crazy, then Jackie Byrne, then the audience.)* Wait a minute. Six rounds, I don't get it?
ROME: They couldn't get Sonny to tank, so they told him he had to kayo Clay before the sixth, cah-peesh? We put just enough on him to kayo Clay before the sixth to make it worthwhile, than we put ah bundle on Clay in the sixth. Anyway, Sonny said he didn't need six, he only needed one but he couldn't do it. Clay *was* too good; believe me. Sonny

even juz dah globs. He *really* hated Clay, cah-peesh Gary?
GREB: Juiced the gloves, when?
ROME: Just before dah fourth round, his corner put 'at liniment-shit all over his globs, Clay was blinded all t'rough the fourth round. But, Sonny still couldn't kayo him, Clay was too fast and he gave it up just before the bell for the seventh. He was outta shape Pally believe me he didn't train for that fight like he shoulda. Youse know Chris Dundee, don' youse, Jackie says his bruddah Angelo managed youse for awhile, is zatrye G-Man, cah-peesh?
GREB: Yeah, I fought for Chris for five, six years. I knew him pretty good, why?
ROME: Chris was from Phillie; he was wid us Pally, cah-peesh G-Man?
GREB: C'mon man, Ali was blinded, just like you said in the fourth and wanted to quit before the fifth, so if Sonny was gonna tank anyway and Angelo knew that, then why …
ROME: Angelo knew nuttin' Pally, it was Chris what knew: why youse t'ink Angelo pushed him out for the fifth, huh? Cause Chris musta tol' 'im he only needed anuddah round to win. Angelo got the message, Pally, he wasn't stoopid, was he? Lis'en, Pally, dah group 'at was promotin' Sonny, which he got his money from, cut a deal wid 'at Louisville group what had Clay under contract and they made a deal, four months before the fight, to have promotional rights to Clay's next fight and paid fifty large for it too, cah-peesh G-Man?
(*Pause*)
GREB: What? If they figured Sonny for a sure winner then why would they do somethin' like …?
ROME: My point exactly Pally; I can see youse ain't too stoopid eithah, cah-peesh?
GREB: Yeah but Chris and Angelo never knew … I mean … hmm ...
ROME: (*Interrupts*) Chris knew Pally; he mighta kept Angelo outta it but he knew, Chris knew. Look Carbo *was* boxin', for a long time, he had the IBC in 'is pocket and the play was to control both dah fighters in any big bout; see we woulda had Clay *and* Sonny but then Clay became

Ali and they couldn't deal wid the Black Muslims. Anyway, the second fight, which they had the promotional rights tah, like I jus' said, Sonny was in better shape, until Clay got the hernia, but we still got good odds and 'at's why they wanted him to tank in ah fois', we got seven to one, like I said, cah-peesh G-Man?

GREB: What'd Sonny get for that fight?

(*Beat.*)

ROME: He got paid big-time but he blew it on ah dames and ah booze. He was broke by the end of the year. Yeah, funny t'ing about Sonny, when he was on top just before he kayoed Patterson everybody wanted him to lose, youse know, he was the bad guy and he took to that, 'cause youse know he *was* a *bad guy* but when he fought Clay, then Ali, everybody wanted him to win and he became the good guy and it was like youse know he couldn't be the good guy. Course that visit he had from the Black Muslims didn't help, see after Clay hadda hernia, Sonny stopped trainin' and these Muslims come around his trainin' camp and tol' him he needed to lose. Like I said, youse couldn't control dem Black Muslims, cah-peesh G-Man?

(*Beat*)

GREB: (*Looks at audience as if there's no end to what Tony Rome will try to get him to believe.*) What? They threatened *Sonny Liston,* hah, man-oh-man.

ROME: Don't laugh Pally, dose Muslims was some scary bastids. Remember, they kilt Malcolm X, cah-peesh Gary?

(*Beat*)

GREB: Look whose talkin'. You guys were scary bastards. C'mon?

ROME: Yeah, but Sonny knew these Muslims from when he was inside; he never bought into dem but he never understood 'em either, he t'ought dey was crazy, cah-peesh? Believe it or not Sonny was the leas' prejudice poy-sun I evah knew, it was Ali and the Muslims dat was prejudice and these Black Muslims was preachin' they was the mastah race, so Sonny jus' t'ought they was crazy and Sonny was a lil' uptight about crazy people. He didn't like dere visit; he t'ought everybody

wanted him to lose 'at fight, cah-peesh G-Man?
(*Pause*)
GREB: (*Raises eyebrows and hands and shakes head.*) Man, the way you tell it Tony, everybody did?
(*Beat*)
ROME: Yeah, poor ol' Sonny, of all my hits, all ah 'em, Sonny's is the one I regret the mos', cah-peesh G-Man?
GREB: (*Looks at Tony Rome's face and sees a stone, with two ice cubes for eyes.*) Yeah, well, how did you, ah-um, *exactly* fulfill the hit? The *contract*?
(*Beat.*)
ROME: He was partyin' wid Mary and she put the powder in 'is drink to knock him out and then I come in a lil' later with the needle and go over to Sonny, see, he's sittin' in 'is chair and pow, he wakes up, cah-peesh?
(*Beat.*)
GREB: What? (*Looks at audience again and shakes his head.*)
(*Beat*)
ROME: Yeah, 'at jah-mook was tough, Mary had given him a triple dose in 'is drink too. Funny t'ing dough, he just sat there while I stuck the needle in his arm and didn't do nuttin', as much as he was scared ah needles, to this day I t'ink he let me do it to him, cah-peesh Gary?
GREB: Yeah, why would he *let you* kill him, c'mon Tony? He didn't know you were …
ROME: No, but he was tired man, real tired. He was tired ah life, youse know tired ah bein' used by everybody. He didn't have the will to live anymore, poor kid, cah-peesh G-Man?
(*Pause*)
GREB: So you *killed* the *poor kid,* huh Tony and maybe you were just doing him a favor then ah, how much you get for clippin' Sonny again?
(*Pause*)
ROME: (*Stares at Greb for about ten seconds and his eyes are cold, hard and calculating. Then, has a coughing fit.*) Ten large, pally, I got ten large for Sonny, cah-peesh G-Man?(*Voice takes on a tone of disgust,*

as he tells how much he had been paid to kill Sonny Liston.)
GREB: How much did you get for Kennedy?
(*Pause*)
ROME: (*Stares at Greb, with eyes like ice-cubes.*) See (*Looks at Jackie Byrne.*) dat's why I pick diz guy fah a writah, 'cause he got balls. See, me too, I had balls. Yeah he'll write dah trood aw'ight. Two hundred and fifty large for Kennedy and, like I said, I got made wid Kennedy, cahpeesh Gary?
GREB: You got a quarter mil' for Kennedy and only ten grand for Sonny?
(*Pause*)
ROME: (*Prolonged silence, then smiles at Greb.*) Yeah, yeh-uh, I like diz kid, man, youse ah aw'ight. Youse ah aw'ight. Look, I owed dem a little somethin' and they forgot my debt for Sonny but, like I said aw'eady, nobody cared about Sonny, it was ah easy hit. And he didn't care anymore, like I said, cah-peesh G-Man?
GREB: Who paid you for the Kennedy killing? *(Pause.)* C'mon Tony, you want me to write your autobiography or not? I need it all?
(*Beat.*)
ROME: Sure, ahacccck, I'll be dead before anybody reads it anyway. I got paid by two different guys, one was a spook, the other was a mob under-boss, cah-peesh Gary?
(*Beat.*)
GREB: (*Looks at audience again, as if Tony is crazy.*) Tony? You're tellin' me you got paid to kill the President of the United States by the mob and by the federal government, the C.I.A., Tony? The spooks paid you? To kill a **SITTING PRESIDENT?**
ROME: (*Pause. Smiles crookedly*) I'm tellin' yah what happened, cahpeesh? The same spooks I worked for in 'Nam recruited me for the Kennedy job, cah-peesh Gary?
GREB: And that was your first hit for the spooks?
(*Beat.*)
ROME: Outside ah dah 'Nam yeah, they wanted me to do Castro when

I had only been in-country a couple months but the spooks had me already signed up to do some woik in Cambodia and Laos. Yeah, diz guy May-hew, dude woiked for Howard Hughes; see he had contacted Roselli about a hit on Castro and the spooks wanted me to do it. Roselli never came across for them and they took him out for it, cah-peesh? *(Beat.)*

GREB: Roselli …?

ROME: John Roselli, a guy I knew before I went in ah crotch, I did some woik for 'im and he got me in with the wiseguys, youse know, back when I'us still jus' a kid, cah-peesh G-Man?

GREB: This guy Roselli, who took 'im out …?

(Beat.)

ROME: The spooks, I t'ink, cah-peesh Gary … ah-hah … awwghhhacck ... *(Goes into a coughing spasm and runs into kitchen)*

(Pause)

GREB: Man, Jackie, this guy might die anytime. Shit!

(Beat.)

BYRNE: *(Stares at Greb.)* What G-Man?

GREB: What? Shit. I shoulda brought my tape player. I shouldah anyway but now? This guy can barely breathe. Dude's maybe ah hundred, hundred-twenty pounds. All those pictures, dude is two and-a-half bills or more. Had a belly like Santa Claus on 'im.

BYRNE: Was is right, he's a buck and a quarter if he's lucky. Where's your tape player?

(Beat)

GREB: I left my briefcase at your house, so …

BYRNE: Yeah youse been doin' the law resoich too long, capeesh? *(Smiles)* Youse hear all diz stuff G-Man? Killed JFK and Sonny Liston. Heh, played no favorites huh?

(Beat.)

GREB: Yeah, y'know what Jackie? I remember a piece in ah paper and check this out? Talk about an ironic twist of fate when it was first announced that Floyd Patterson would defend his title against Sonny, back in sixty-two, JFK calls Patterson in to the White House and counsels him that he *must beat that thug,* Sonny Liston.

BYRNE: No shit? Man, and Tony clipped 'em both?

GREB: Ain't that a bitch? Hey, here he comes. Hey Tony, how're yah feelin'? (*Tony Rome walks slowly, the oxygen tank in his hands, the tubes in his nose, and sits down.*)

(*Pause*)

ROME: I wish I wuz dead but I'm onah stay alive to tell diz story, cah-peesh G-Man?

(*Pause*)

GREB: Yeah, uh-ah, I was just tellin' Jackie about an ironic twist of fate, a historical twist of fate, y'know, when it was first announced that Floyd Patterson would defend his title against Sonny, back in sixty-two, JFK called Patterson in to the White House and counseled him that he hadda *beat that thug,* Sonny Liston.

ROME: Sure, I knew dat, everybody, like I said before Pally, wanted Patterson to beat Sonny. Know what Sonny called 'im?

GREB: Called who? Kennedy?

ROME: No Floyd Patterson, Sonny called him Patsy, hahherah, cah-peesh Gary?

(Beat)

GREB: Oh yeah? Ain't that about the same thing you called Oswald, Tony?

(*Pause*)

ROME: (*Scowls at Greb's ironic retort, then reaches for his wine glass and drains it quickly. He pours another one and is spilling it when Jackie Byrne steadies his hand and it fills his glass.*) T'anks Jackie. It's the only t'ing I got to look forward to anymore, youse know, a lil vino every now and then, cah-peesh Jackie? And a cigarette but just one, foist t'ing inna mawnin', youse know?

GREB: You know Tony I can't understand how you guys got away with this for so many years?

(*Beat*)

ROME: Ehhh. It's all bullshit and money, cah-peesh Gary … Jackie?
(*Beat*.)
GREB: Bullshit and money? What ah you mean by that?
ROME: Just that, Pally, we'd t'row up a smokescreen and t'row enough money aroun' to everybody had any interest in it, cah-peesh? Course there was always guys that knew, cah-peesh Gary … Jackie?
(*Pause Greb and Byrne exchange bemused looks*.)
GREB: Guys that knew? Like who?
ROME: Dere's always some spooks and some mob guys what know.
GREB: Yeah, you wanna give me some names? You know Tony, it looks like the spooks and the mob had a lot in common?
ROME: The spooks couldn't be trusted,
(*Beat*.)
GREB: Wha' … ah … uht? And the mob could?
ROME: Of course. We have Omerta?
GREB: Tell that to Joe Valachi, huh?
(*Beat*.)
ROME: (*Face turns grim, you can see he is fuming*.) A rat, a rat. I don't want to talk about Valachi; it gives me agita, cah-peesh guys? (*Looks at Greb and then at Jackie Byrne, as if Greb is not showing him enough respect*.)
GREB: They got a lotta mob guys givin' people up nowadays, the witness protection program, yah know?
(*Beat*)
ROME: We still have Omerta, believe me, now let's talk about sumpin' else, you wanna know about JFK or maybe Sonny or whatever but I don't wanna get heartboin, cah-peesh guys?
GREB: Sonny Liston and J.F.K., two guys at opposite ends of the spectrum, huh?
BYRNE: Yeah, they sure were.
(*Pause*)
ROME: Wait a minute now, lemme tell youse sumpin', dose two guys was a lot alike.

GREB: A lot alike, what're you jokin'? He must be jokin' huh Jackie?
BYRNE: (*Looks at Tony Rome questioningly.*) I dunno? Tony?
(*Beat*)
ROME: Youse know what Sonny said after he lost the first Clay fight?
GREB: What? (*Glances at Jackie Byrne, who is smiling*)
ROME: Said he never felt as bad since J.F.K. had been shot.
GREB: Hah, and you clipped 'em both huh Tony?
(*Beat.*)
ROME: Yeah, I wish I hadn't hoit Sonny like that."
GREB: (*Exchanges bemused smiles with Byrne.*) Man, you got more remorse for Liston than Kennedy, Tony?
(*Beat*)
ROME: (*Hard, cold eyes soften for just an instant.*) I always liked Sonny youse know, I mean he was really misunderstood, cah-peesh guys?
(*Beat*)
GREB: Tony, John Kennedy was the President of the United States? He saved us all during the Cuban Missile Crisis. I know, I was in the Corps at that time and the alert was insane at P.I. C'mon Tony?
(*Beat.*)
ROME: Yeah and youse know what? Him and Sonny, like I said, was a lot alike, they was both hounds youse know? Kennedy couldn't leave the broads alone and neither could Sonny. And, also, youse know, both ah 'em went to the top ah their professions. Kennedy was President and Sonny was the Heavyweight World Champeen and he was a tough bastid, I knew 'im good too, cah-peesh Gary? Wha' jah expect from a black kid born in Alabama durin' a time dey hung you fo' bein' black and his old man beat on him everyday too. Like I said, I knew Sonny, I used to go fishin' wid him in a little lake see ... ahaaaccck, ah hooo ... (*Starts a coughing fir again.*)
GREB: (*Looks at Jackie, who shakes his head.*) You aw'rye Tony? Look, you got a point there, Tony but how about you tell me about how you whacked Martin Luther King, Junior now?

(*Pause*)
ROME: I killed King. Aaaaccckkk (*Begins another steady staccato of tubercular coughs that only end when he finally gets the hoses up his nose and begins a slow, sustained staccato of gulping breaths until finally, he is breathing normally again, or as normally as could be expected for someone with terminal lung cancer.*) Yeah, I did King, youse know and it was easier than Kennedy, much easier.
GREB: Wait a minute; what about that James Earl Ray guy?
ROME: Annudder patsy, youse kiddin' me, cah-peesh? (*His face is a very pale white.*)
GREB: How about Jimmy Hoffa …? You clip him too?
ROME: Niente, but I know who did, cah-peesh?
(*Beat*)
GREB: (*Looks into audience again, skeptically.*) Aother mob hitman?
ROME: Nullo, nu … acahhhaccckkkk. (*Goes into yet another sustained period of coughing and has to get another oxygen tank from his bedroom and motions for Greb and Byrne to follow him when he gets his breathing back enough to speak again.*) Come back tomorrow, it's gettin' late, it's too late, cah-peesh? Gary? Jackie
GREB: (*Looks at his watch and sees it is past midnight and motions to Jackie, who nods.*) Okay then Tony, tomorrow. Look I'm gonna bring my tape recorder tomorrow and you're gonna give me these names, okay.
ROME: (*Nods his head and smiles.*) Yeah, no problem, I'll even let you in on who shot Hoffa, cah-peesh G-Man?
GREB: (*Shakes hands with Rome.*) Great stuff Tony. See yah tomorrow.
ROME: (*Laughs.*) Sure, I know youse'll be back tomorrow, I wasn't made wid a finger, cah-peesh guys?
GREB: (*Shakes hands with Rome, as does Byrne.*) Okay Tony, see yah. (*Greb and Byrne walk to the front door and exit. They hear Rome slide the deadbolt in place, on the other side of the door and light fades..*)

INTERMISSION

ACT III

SCENE 1

Setting: Next day, Jackie Byrne's house; kitchen table.

GREB: Man, Jackie, I didn't sleep very good last night.
BYRNE: No G-Man? Why not? I slept like a baby.
GREB: I had this weird freakin' dream man and I can't explain it?
(*Beat*)
BYRNE: Dream? Can't explain it? What the fugg youse talkin' 'bout G-Man? Here, Maria cooked us some scrambled eggs and she got orange juice and coffee and toast.
(*Pause*)
GREB: (*Looks at table set with plates and glasses and cups for coffee.*) Okay, lemme think a little first. I had a rough night, couldn't sleep. Today's Sunday Jackie. We should go to church?
(*Pause*)
BYRNE: G-Man? Are youse kiddin'? Marie and the kids already went, youse shouldah said sumpin'. I mean, c'mon, fuggin' Tony Rome could die any minute man? I mean, youse wanna go and get this guy's story or what? He could fuggin' die, I'm tellin' yah. Like youse din' see dah skelton he is? Diz muhfuh he could …
GREB: Stop cursin' man.
(*Pause*)
BYRNE: Wha … wha ..ah … uht? What the fugg's mattah wid chew? Since when did youse ever give a fugg about doity woids? Youse'ave put me to shame many times wid yah mouth, c'mon G-Man. What dah fuggs wid diz dream? Yah losin' yah mind ah what?
(*Beat*)
GREB: I, I dreamt it was 1966 and I was back in Vegas: I was in Bill

Miller's gym, it was just under this restaurant he owned and all these guys I knew was there, Ralph Dupas and Ferd and …
BYRNE: G-man Ferd-dah?
GREB: Yeah, Ferd Hernandez and Johnny Little was there, 'at's Freddie's brother me and him was pals and …
BYRNE: G-Man, what's wid diz story, sounds weird man?
(*Pause*)
GREB: (*Looks at Byrne and shakes his head. Takes a piece of toast and butters it, then takes a bite and a sip of orange juice.*) Gimme a break man, I tol' jew it *was* weird. Let me talk.
BYRNE: (*Shakes his head and put his hands out, palms upward.*) Go ahead BoDiddley.
(*Beat*)
GREB: Okay, so all these guys, like Andy Kendall, Joe Clark, Benny Juarez, Larry Clark, Candy Barnes are there in the gym and we was all like shadow-boxin' and in come Sonny and he …
BYRNE: Liston? (*Smiles at Greb and the audience and sips at coffee*)
(*Pause*)
GREB: Yeah, Liston. Anyway, he comes in followed by his trainer and another fighter. The trainer informs us that Sonny and his sparring partner needed the ring and we all quickly vacate it. Liston and his sparring partner had barely gone a round when Liston catches him with a short left hook and he goes down, unconscious. They take him out on a stretcher and the next thing I know I'm doing my sit-ups and I look over and Liston is skipping rope to *Wipeout*, a drum solo that he had playing on a small record player that was sitting on the floor. I saw that he was giving me the evil eye, something I never took from nobody and I wasn't about to start now, Sonny Liston or no Sonny Liston.
BYRNE: Yeah, I remember when youse took dat golfcart that Ali was drivin' down in Miami Beach. Man, G-Man, you are a crazy muhfuh ain't no question 'bout dat. Go on wid dah dream.
(*Beat*)
GREB: Okay, so ah-num-er-um-ah, where was I, so Liston was starin' at

me yah know and so I glare back at 'im and then I nod at him and look around the gym and saw that everybody else was gone. So, I finish my sit-ups and go into the dressing room to shower and so, I'm takin' a shower when suddenly the shower curtain is ripped open and I'm staring into the menacing, scowling face of Sonny Liston. I was really startled Jackie but I eyeball him back, again, and he like laughs and says to me that we should spar a few rounds maybe the next day. And, I'm like kinna dumb-founded but I tell 'im sure I'll box wid 'im the nex' day. So, I get outta the shower and while I'm gettin' dressed Sonny's starin' at me and he tells me this lame joke and I just shake my head and don't laugh or nothin' and his face has metamorphosed in a heartbeat and he's scowling at me like a muhfuh shaking me for a second Jackie I can still remember the blood drainin' from my face when I saw his eyes go cold and hard like two icicles, then, just as suddenly, they turned softer and became kind and friendly and warm. And he says to me like, hey G-Man you know man we're friends ain't we G-Man?
BYRNE: Wha' … ah … uht? C'mon G-Man, Sonny Liston says to you ain't we friends?
(*Beat.*)
GREB: (*exasperatingly, pissed off at Byrne.*) C'mon Jack-off, it's just a freakin' dream man, a *dream.*
BYRNE: Yeah, oh yeah-yeah, sure G-Man. Weird dream G-Man. (*Looks at audience.*) Weird dream, huh?
(*Pause*)
GREB: (*Smiles now and shakes his head.*) So, get this, he sticks out his hand to me and says: Hey, I love yah G-Man.
BYRNE: G-Man, youse sayin' Sonny Liston was a sissy? (*Shakes head and looks at audience.*)
GREB: (*Obviously mad, shakes his head and stands up.*) Damn man, you nuts Jack-off. C'mon if I tell yah I love you am I a faggot?
(*Pause*)
BYRNE: (*Smiling.*) Hahah, I know man he ain't a sissy. Sounds like a lonely dude though man, y'know G-Man? No real friends.

GREB: Yeah, everybody was usin' him, y'know, makin' money off him and shit.
(B*eat.*)
BYRNE: Yeah, so what'd he do? In yah dream? (*Sarcastically, looks at audience and put his hands out palms up.*)
(*Beat.*)
GREB: Okay man, so his hand is stuck out towards me and I'm in a state of shock. All the times I trained in the gym with him and he hadn't bothered to say two words to anybody, much less any kind words, and now, out of the blue, this. So, I shake hands with him but then suddenly inexplicably, his eyes metamorphosed yet again and became cold and hard, just like I had always seen them in the gym. He squeezes my hand hard and it felt like it was in a vice and I frown and then his eyes turn soft again but then, just as quickly, they went hard again. He was just about to say something to me when I woke up. Y'know, it's freezing outside, and I had one of the windows open, but, nevertheless, I was sweatin'. It like ran across my face and down my neck and my right hand was pulsating and like kinna numb.
BYRNE: G-Man, you're goin' nutzoid. Have some more orange juice.
GREB: I know man but wanna hear somethin' even weirder?
(*Pause*)
BYRNE: (*Looks at audience, skeptically.*) I don't tha … think so G-Man. (*Sarcastically, raises coffee-cup and sips.*)
(*Pause*)
GREB: Jackie, his eyes man, his eyes.
(*Pause*)
BYRNE: (*Looks at audience and puts his hands out, palms up.*) Eyes G-Man? Who … ah whose eyes is it youse ah zactlee talk'in 'bout here?
(*Beat.*)
GREB: Jackie, Sonny Liston's eyes.
(*Pause*)
BYRNE: (*Shakes head and looks at audience as if he should have known.*) Of course; Sonny Liston's eyes, hah, how stoopid ah me.

(*Pause*)

GREB: Yeah, whose do you think they looked like? Huh?

(*Pause*)

BYRNE: Ah-er, num-ah-er … Whose ah-er … whose what are we … (*Looks at audience.*) Are we …

(*Pause.*)

GREB: Jackie, Sonny Liston's eyes man. Whose do you think they looked like? (*Glares at Byrne, as if he hasn't been listening to him or he'd know the answer.*)

(*Beat.*)

BYRNE: (*Looks at audience, shrugging at them and putting his hands, palms up towards them, as if asking for their help.*) Okay G-Man. Whose eyes do Sonny Liston's eyes look like? Right?

GREB: Right! (*Obviously mad, again*)

BYRNE: Whose ah-nah-um-ah … whose ah eyes look like … ah-er … like whose eyes look like his eyes?

(*Beat.*)

GREB: Right. (*Says it and looks at Byrne as if he's an idiot who finally figured out how to put a square peg into a square hole and at the audience, in their battle to get the audience on their side.*)

(*Beat.*)

BYRNE: I dunno G-Man, y'know? Whose eyes Sonny's eyes look like?

GREB: Tony's Jackie, Tony Rome's eyes man. They're cold and look like icicles all the time. Don't tell me you don't notice that. His eyes are cold man, cold as a killer's, which he is.

(*Pause*)

BYRNE: (*Shakes head and stares at audience.*) G-Man, I shouldah known, yeah, yeah, you're right dere. I been knowin' dat guy for years man, everybody in the neighborhood knows he's connected and a made guy and yeah, youse know, come to think ah it (*Turns to audience and smiles widely.*) they always say his eyes are like icicles G-Man, just like icicles.

(*Beat.*)

GREB: (*Drinks remainder of glass of orange juice.*) Aw-ight Bo-Jack, I got my recorder. (*Holds up tape player and stands up.*) Let's roll over to Tony Rome's?
BYRNE: I'm comin' man but it's freezin' out, let's get our coats?

SCENE 2

Setting: Tony Rome in front of his house, scraping a frozen car window.

GREB: (*Walking out the front door, lights come up as they see Tony Rome, just down the street, in front of his house, scraping the frozen ice off his car's windshield.*) Looks like he's scraping the ice off his short what dah hell's he doin' that for in this kinna weather Jackie?
(*Pause*)
BYRNE: I dunno G-Man. Gee-zuz, G-Man, Gee-zuz …? (*Both men have stopped and are staring straight ahead, where Tony Rome has fallen on the ground.*)
(*Pause*)
GREB: What the fuh ..(*Runs towards Tony Rome and finds him lying on the snow-filled ground, in front of his car. Bends down and cradles his head in his hands. Sees a lit cigarette on Rome's coat*) Tony, you aw'ight man, Tony? Man Jackie, dude was smokin' a cigarette?
(*Pause*)
BYRNE: (*Stands a few feet away and Greb looks up at him. Rome's face is as white as the snow.*) I'll go call nine-one-one.
(*Beat.*)
GREB: You got one ah those new portable phones. Cell-phones?
(*Pause*)
BYRNE: Naw-ah, they ain't no good, I'll go call nine-one-one. (*Runs

back to his house and disappears in wings.)
GREB: *(Notices that Tony Rome's forehead is bloody and gets blood on his coat and hands.)* Tony, you aw'ight man? What happened man? *(Pause)*
ROME: I fell G-Man, I, this, this huge pain in my chest man, my side, my legs went to jelly. I, I shouldah skipped my mawnin' cigarette but it clears my head and I can breathe better too, for awhile. Shh, I had a heart attack again. I remember what the doctor tol' me. I'm really stoopid. G-Man, do youse believe in ah soul?
GREB: Yeah Tony, I do believe in the soul. I do.
(Beat.)
ROME: Youse know what? *(Rasps so scratchy can barely be heard.)* *(Pause)*
GREB: What? What Tony? I can't hear you?
(Pause)
ROME: Wha … uh .. Forgive me man, please forgive me, please? *(Holds a cross and a rosary in his hands and begins to cry, sobbing, at first very low and, gradually louder.)*
(Pause)
GREB: Tony I'll get a priest, I'll get a …
(Beat.)
ROME: *(Grips his coat tightly and pulls on it to pull himself up a few inches, closer to Greb's face.)* Forgive me, please? Please forgive me? I … I gotta be forgiven, youse kin forgive … I know you can?
(Pause)
GREB: Tony, there's a priest just down the street, at your church, Jackie tol' me you go to the same church; Our Lady ah Grace and I can get a priest, maybe one you know and …
ROME: *(Pulls himself up again and is only inches from Greb's face.)* No! No priest. I need forgiveness, **NOW!** Forgive me, please forgive me?
GREB: Tony, forgive you? I can't; I, I ain't a priest?
(Beat.)

ROME: Please forgive me, please, I can't die like diz ... if you don't forgive me? Please, please, Gee-zuz, please forgive me? (*Starts crying, very low, and then louder until he screams, like a madman:*) **FORGIVE ME!**
(*Pause*)
GREB: Tony, I ain't a priest? How can I ... ?
(*Pause*)
ROME: Forgive me please for hoitin' Sonny like dat ... for hoitin ... dah country and for ...
GREB: Tony, my God, your eyes, your eyes are. You're ... you're forgiven Tony, you're forgiven. Do you hear me? **I FORGIVE YOU!** (*Tony Rome's eyes turn soft and his face relaxes, as he slumps backwards.*)
(*Pause*)
BYRNE: (*Can be heard running onto the scene, talks like he's out of breath.*) I called 'em, they're on their way.
(*Pause*)
GREB: I just forgave him man, do you believe that? Like I could *forgive* anybody for their actions on earth, but the guy was beggin' me, he was cryin', pleadin' with me to ... Holy Jesus, God almighty, look, look at his eyes, Jackie? Hey Tony, man, hold on, the ambulance and the paramedics are on their way.
BYRNE: Gee-zuz, G-Man, lookit 'is eyes. He's gone man.
(*Pause*)
GREB: (*Puts Rome's head down on the snow and puts his ear against his chest, then grabs his wrist. Thirty seconds and he lets it go.*) No pulse Jackie. He's gone.
(*Pause*)
GREB: (*Stands up, as does Byrne.*) Did you see his eyes?
(*Pause*)
BYRNE: (*Shaking.*) It was an optical illusion G-Man.
(*Pause*)
GREB: (*Puts face an inch from Byrne's.*) Did you **SEE HIS EYES?**

JACKIE, DID YOU ... SEE HIS EYES? (*Screaming.*)
(*Beat.*)
BYRNE: (*Shaking and stuttering.*) Looked like icicles frozen on 'em and they fell off. Like, c'mon G-Man, it's freezing out here. I saw them ... I saw them ... youse know ... ice ... ah-er-um ... ice ... ice melts? Dah ... don't it?
(*Pause*)
GREB: (*Obviously mad, glares at Byrne and puts his face back to within an inch.*) Jackie, I seen those eyes in my dream. They were Tony's the whole time until the very end, when you bent down and we both saw them and Jackie, (*Holds hand up in the air and stutters*) I swear to God, Jackie, I saw, I swear they were the same eyes I saw last night in my dream! **I SWEAR TO GOD** (*looks upward and holds his hand upwards towards the sky; his voice cracks.*) Jackie, they were **SONNY LISTON'S EYES.**

END OF PLAY
(BLACKOUT OR CURTAIN.)

BAD MEDICINE

AN ORIGINAL PLAY IN TWO ACTS & A REQUIEM

CHARACTERS:

TERESA STEIN: 31-year-old freelance writer.
Dr. SAMUEL BERGER: Doctor and friend of Stein's from college. Age 30-40.
BETTY CUSHER: Owner of We Care Age 30-50.
TERRY McCALLUM: LPN working as an RN Age 25-35.
BARBARA BILLING: Nurse in training Age 25-35
Dr. PETER PAULSON: Chief surgeon at Long General, has a fictitious medical degree. Age 50-60.
LINDA BLACK: Pharmacy Technician with no training. Age 18.
GINA ZERBA: An LPN masquerading as an anesthesiologist. Age 25-35.
Dr. ANTHONY HALL: Private Practice Doctor. Age 30-50.
WANDA WADE: Wife of Tim Wade, a patient at Long General Age 30-50
ELLEN CREWS: Head Nurse at Long General Age 35-45
MAITRE d': Age 25-45
JUDY COLLINS: Respiratory Therapist Age 25-35
ORDERLY: Age 25-35.
Dr. STANLEY CRUSHHORN: Anesthesiologist, also an alcoholic. Age 55-70

ACT I
6 SCENES

We see into We Care, a temporary service that provides medical workers to privately-run local hospitals, where we also see into the workers' lives and how they got there and how they are performing in these temporary jobs, in the medical *battlegrounds of* South Florida's, privately owned and operated hospitals.

ACT 1   SCENES and SETTINGS

SCENE 1: DOCTOR'S OFFICE-Doctor prescribes pain killers.
SCENE 2: TERESA STEIN'S APARTMENT
SCENE 3: BUSINESS OFFICE
SCENE 4: HOSPITAL CAFETERIA
SCENE 5: DOCTOR'S OFFICE
SCENE 6: HOSPITAL

ACT II
4 SCENES

We see the results and ramifications of the temp workers.

SCENE 1: RESTAURANT
SCENE 2: HOSPITAL ROOM
SCENE 3: HOSPITAL PHARMACY
SCENE 4: HOSPITAL ROOM

REQUIEM: VOICE FROM HOSPITAL

ACT I

SCENE 1

Setting: A doctor's office.

TERESA STEIN: (*Smiles at Dr. Sam Berger, a former classmate of hers at NYU. Stein is a free-lance writer, working on a half-finished novel and Berger, who had once dated her, was well-aware that she had a deadline to meet within the next week.*) Sam, I'm just tired.
(*Beat.*)
BERGER: Teresa, you're more than just tired, aren't you?
(*Beat.*)
STEIN: (*Smiles at Berger, almost ghoulishly.*) I'm exhausted Sammy.
BERGER: Does your breakup with Steve have anything to do with it?
(*Pause.*)
STEIN: Well, it *certainly* doesn't help any? And, I am depressed a lot of the time too Sam. And my work is suffering, I need to finish my book on deadline or I'll lose a big bonus. Can you give me something or not?
(*Beat.*)
BERGER: For your depression … or for … ?
STEIN: I need *something* Sam.
BERGER: I can give you some Nardil and I think it might help. Just be sure to follow the instructions and don't drink or take any other medications, alright Tee?
STEIN: (*Smiles, thinking maybe she has found an answer, finally.*) Surely I won't Sam, surely I won't. (*Light fades stage left, comes up on stage right.*)

SCENE 2

Setting: Teresa Stein's apartment, in Ft. Lauderdale.

TERESA STEIN: (*Sitting at her word processor, she stares at the blank screen, wondering where she is at in the story. She glances at a small plastic container that houses the pills that her doctor had prescribed for her*: *15 milligram tablets that she was to take three times a day. Reaches for the container and stares at it absently. She's been taking them for two weeks and the result has been to calm her nerves enough so that she is on the last chapter in her book and a $50,000 bonus awaits her last word. She is agitated and stares at the pill container, wondering when she had last taken one, as Berger has doubled her dose after she complains of an increased amount of stress that she is experiencing as she gets closer to finishing her novel. As she stares at the small container of Phenelzine, her agitation turns to confusion and her forehead becomes shiny with sweat, while her fingers begin sticking to each other and she can't write with clammy hands and damp skin. She reaches for the container, twists off the cap, and pops a tablet into her mouth, then reaches for a glass of water and frowns when it isn't where she had thought it to be. Stands up and her head begins spinning, even as her heart begins pounding irregularly. She has an immense craving for something sweet and remembers that there is some leftover cake in her refrigerator. She quickly retrieves it, but, as she sits down to eat the cake, she tries to remember what food restrictions come with her prescription, the same prescription she had just been re-reading, as a new one had been enclosed with her new prescription but now she couldn't remember where she had put it. She stands up.*) Damn it, why can't I remember anything? (*Stumbles and falls down.*)

SCENE 3

Setting: Business office. (*Light comes up on stage right.*)

BETTY CUSHER: (*Cusher is the founder and CEO of We Care, a temporary nursing agency, located just outside of Ft. Lauderdale. Sitting in office when phone rings.*) Hello We Care this is Betty. What? You need an RN for the eleven to seven. I'll send one over. What? Her name? Ah, Terry, Terry McCallum. Fine. (*She pushes another blinking line.*) We Care, hold please. (*She pushes yet another blinking line.*) Okay, this is Betty, how can I help you? An RN for the grave-yard. I'll send one over, what? Her name, ah-nah Barbara, Barbara Billing. Okay. (*She pushes the other line but they had hung up already.*) Muh-fuh, damn to fuggin' hell, muh-fuh'ahs can't even hold for … ah-eh. (*Cusher hates to lose any business. She quickly stabs out seven numbers.*) Terry, I need you for an eleven-seven shift, yes; Long General.

TERRY McCALLUM: (*Looks exhausted*) Can't do it Bets, I just came off a sixteen-hour shift.

BETTY CUSHER: Damnit Bets, I need you, they need an RN and I … (*Beat*)

TERRY: Betty you know I'm an LPN?

BETTY: Girl, I tol' jew before, jus' show up. I'll, I'll give you a fifty-dollar bonus, cash money, now get over to Long by eleven tonight. (*Beat*)

TERRY: That's only six hours from now and I'm dead Bets. (*Beat*)

BETTY: I'll make it seventy-five and get you a steady by next week. No, really; I got a six-month straight gig in Miami … yes … yes and they pay as much for you, an LPN, as an RN gets at Long.

TERRY: All right then but I hope it works out because I'm awful tired.

BETTY: Good girl, got another call.

(*Beat*)
TERRY: (*Stares at a dead-line and looks at the clock again.*) Damn her, hell, what's smattah with me anyway, she never comes through with any of her bullshit promises. I'd better get some shut-eye.
(*Beat*)
BETTY: (*Stabs out seven numbers.*) Hello, Barb, I need you for a graveyard. What? Don't worry about that, just show up. Uh, Long General, yeah, yeah I know but, look there's a steady opening coming up at Mt. Sinaii, yeah, next month and I'll get you on. What? Six months, leads to permanent. C'mon, Mt. Sinaii's top-shelf, nothin' like Long. Okay, I got you down for it. Look, I know you haven't finished school yet but they don't check, don't worry, it's good training for you y'know? Real, not classroom. On, come on, I did it myself before I got my nursing license. And, you said yourself, you only need one more semester and you'll have it by the time the Mt. Sinaii gig comes up. (*Looks up, on the wall, at a degree in nursing from a school in the Bahamas that she had paid fifty bucks for*) Nothin' ever happens on the graveyard anyway, right sweetie? Oops, got an incoming call, bye sweetie and thanks.
(*Beat*)
BARBARA BILLING: This better be real, that woman lies so much I can't believe she still has a nose.
(*Beat*)
BETTY: Hello, this is Betty. You need three Rn's and one LPN tomorrow at Scared Heart Memorial. Got it, they'll be there.(*Cusher disconnects and is already on another line to another one of her nurses, replicating the conversation she had just had with Barbara McCallum to another nurse. Cusher is being paid handsomely to provide temporary nursing care to dozens of hospitals and nursing homes around the state and, with an annual gross income of three-million dollars, she will provide that care, one way or another, and at any and all costs.*)

SCENE 4

Setting: Long General's cafeteria.(*Light comes up center stage.*) The cafeteria has many customers, the hospital staff eats there for free and we zero in on certain of the people there. A light comes up on a man who is between 50-60 years old and has a medical coat on with a nameplate that identifies him as a doctor. The light spotlights him and he turns towards the audience and speaks.

DR. PETER PAULSON: Oh hello, I'm Doctor Peter Paulsen. I was a medic in Vietnam for two tours an I was wounded, taking shrapnel in my head, neck and back. I attended medical school for almost a year but I just couldn't concentrate, see because I kept getting flashbacks of the Nam, along with my wounds, it just limited my ability to earn the medical degree that I had decided to get before I went to Vietnam, see, so what I did was I quit medical school and traveled overseas for several months, drinking and spending all my money. Well, late one night in Manila, in the Philippines, I bought me a medical degree for two-hundred pesos, ah-eh, about five bucks American, heh-heh, on Recto Street, from a counterfeiter who, for another two-hundred pesos, gave me an internship at a large hospital in Manila, with enough stamps, seals, praises, recommendations and signatures than any one human being could ever have reasonably been expected to receive but, man, you know, I got 'em. Well, I didn't never pay them no heed, see, just threw 'em in my suitcase and stayed drunk for the better part of a year before I decided, just after 9/11 that I was gonna make an attempt to use these forged documents see, so I sent copies of my sealed diplomas, official praises and glowing recommendations to a large hospital in Florida, that was so desperate for doctors that they advertised in medical journals. Yeah, that's unusual so anyway, I realized that you know there must be a real, severe shortage of doctors. I was drunk when I sent an application in but I was sober when I received the answer. Yeah, they told me to report, posthaste, to Long General, where I was gonna be the chief surgeon, being as I, you understand got all these glowing letters of recommendation and such sterling qualifications, which y'know they never checked out, 'cause if they had ah I wouldn't be here now, heh-heh, lookin' at these young vixens in here. Man, they see I'm chief surgeon and they practically pull their dresses over their heads and say **OPERATE.** (*Puts hands out as if pleading with the audience to see his point of view.*) I mean, I know my credentials are blatant forgeries but I, y'know, I got 3 years on the battlefield of Vietnam and, yeah, I might make a ah-nah-um-ah, mistake but … but, c'mon even ah-er, educated doctors make mistakes don't they? I mean I'm a veteran. You … you'd let me operate on you, wouldn't you? (*Turns to audience with his hands out pleading and smiles a carnivorous smile. Light fades away from him and comes up on a young woman, Linda Black, aged 18.*)

LINDA BLACK: (*Turns to the audience and smiles.*) Oh, hi, I'm Linda and I'm a pharmacy technician, see, I helps pharmacists do their job, even though I never had any pharmacological training whatsoever. Mostly, I just hand out pills that I bag from a large supply in the pharmacy, here at Long General, and I perform other ah-er, menial jobs at the pharmacist's request. I'm eighteen years old and I quit high school in the tenth grade but Bett, y'know Betty Cusher,, she owns We Care, y'know, well, she, she told me not to say that and to say I got a Ge-E-Dee but well, I flunked it three times already and I mean I'm not really interested in pharmaceutical work, you know it's really boring but it's easy, all I gotta do is hand out pills, hah, see what could go wrong? I mean, I've been employed here, at Long General for three months already and I know, 'cause I heard some people in the office talkin' that they need to cut labor costs and lighten the exhausted staff pharmacists' work load's, hee-hee, it's actually kinna fun, hee-hee-hee. (*Giggles and puts hand over mouth.*) That's what I do, I guess lighten their work-loads. (*Light fades away and shines upon a young woman aged 25-35.*)

GINA ZERBA: (*Turns towards audience and smiles.*) Oh hi, I'm Gina, Gina Zerba and I'm an LPN but Bett, you know, Betty Cusher at We Care, well, she bribed me to take this duty as an anesthesiologist, which is actually just a certified registered nurse specializing in anesthesiology and I know about it because I assisted several times but I really hope I don't have to do anything tonight, I mean, it's been awhile. (*She smiles at the audience but then frowns.*) Oh please, don't look at me like that? I mean, haven't you ever done **ANYTHING** dishonest in your lives? Look, I do have a two-year degree, after all and I've been working in hospitals for five years now. I mean I'm making an extra hundred tonight and, and, well, I do have a child to support, the father, an RN, the bastard, flew the coop, he's somewhere in Puerto Rico right now, jerk. Oh, please, it'll be alright, believe me, hee-hee, I've done it twice before. (*Smiles at audience as light darkens and appears on Terry McCallum.*)

TERRY McCOLLUM: (*Smiles at audience.*) I'm really just an LPN but I'm an RN tonight, hee-hee but well, I mean, Betty Cusher bribes me with these shifts so what can I do, I mean I do need, I mean, we all need money, more money than we have, I mean I'm so busy I just can't find the time to stick to my diet and I need to lose some weight and I know this doctor and he'll take my insurance and a hundred bucks to take off thirty on my waist and butt and add it to my breasts and … well … stop looking at me **LIKE THAT!.** It's not my fault. It's the system, I mean, well, I mean I have to look good to … look I pay five-hundred a month for this damn insurance and I work for the hospital I need this. (*Smiles at audience as light brightens the entire room and we see several hospital employees, including all the aforementioned frauds, eating and talking, as the stage slowly goes dark.*)

SCENE 5

Setting: Doctor's office. (*Light comes up center stage.*)

Dr. ANTHONY HALL: (*Smiles at Mrs. Wanda Wade, comforting her as best he could. Her husband, a diabetic for three decades, has blood poisoning in his left leg and was scheduled to have it amputated that evening, at Long General.*) I foresee no problems Mrs. Wade.
(*Beat*)
WANDA WADE: Do you know the surgeon, Doctor Hall?
ANTHONY HALL: I know Doctor Stemway is on shift there tonight and he's a fine surgeon, I went to med-school with him.
WANDA WADE: Oh that's good—can—can I go and see Tim tonight?
Dr. ANTHONY HALL: Well Wanda, his surgery's scheduled for nine. I could call over for you, or you could go over, if you wish?
(*Beat*)
WANDA WADE: No, no that's not necessary, I want to go.
Dr. ANTHONY HALL: Well, okay then—I'll try to drop in later in the evening, myself.
WANDA WADE: Oh, thank you so much Doctor.
Dr. ANTHONY HALL: (*Stands up, smiles.*) No problem Missus Wade, none at all. (*Light fades away.*)

SCENE 6

Setting: Long General (*Light comes up and stops on Ellen Crews in the hallway of the Long General.*)

ELLEN CREWS: (*Smiles at audience.*) Oh, hello. I'm Ellen Crews and I am the CNO, that is I am the Chief Nursing Officer here in Long General. I'm the head nurse, okay? I have a Master's Degree in the Science of Nursing and the majority of my staff are underpaid and overworked but I can do nothing about that; I have little or no say in the hiring tactics of this hospital. I've only been here for a little over a year but I'm ready to move on to another hospital. I'm telling you they use so many temp workers now I can't keep track from day to day and I see so many reliable and qualified nurses and doctors quitting because the hospital administration sets our pay so low and our hours so long, along with their attitudes on the quality of the care we deliver. They just do not care about the quality of care: they focus strictly on the rate of pay and cost-cutting is their number one priority. I'm fulfilling a life-long desire to help people but I wonder now if this is possible anymore, especially in such a volatile environment as Long General, where germs here just spread so quickly and pervasively that many healthy people visiting here return as patients, catching a virus here, at the very institution they return to, seeking a cure. (*Coughs*) Oh, the flu is everywhere in this hospital and you can't even walk the corridors as I do without inhaling them and, even though I just had a flu shot, some of these germs are immune to any medications, and they make their way into my lungs and nostrils. (*Emits short hacking coughs.*) See what I mean. (*Sees Dr. Paulsen coming down the hallway and turns away from the audience and toward him. She stops him and puts her hand on his forearm.*) Oh, Doctor Paulsen, there is a patient in the operating room.

Dr. PETER PAULSON: Doctor Stemway is the attending physician tonight, Nurse Crews.

ELLEN CREWS: Sir, Doctor Stemway had a heart attack this afternoon and is in surgery at this very moment—at Mt. Sinaii.

Dr. PETER PAULSON: (*Frowns. In the month he had been there, he hadn't had to do anything, even though he was the chief surgeon, other than give advice and be available to assist the attending physician, or to supervise.*) Well, ah-nah-um …

ELLEN CREWS: Doctor, you're the only surgeon in the hospital and this patient has been waiting since nine and it's now eleven.

Dr. PETER PAULSON: Well, what are we waiting for then? Hah! Let's go nurse. Hah! Lead the way—I will operate **MYSELF!**"

INTERMISSION
(BLACKOUT OR CURTAIN)

ACT II
SCENE 1

Setting: Fine dining Restaurant. (*Light comes up, showing a few tables behind Teresa Stein, who has just entered the restaurant.*)

TERESA STEIN: (*Smiles at the maitre d', who returns it.*) Just myself. (*Beat.*)
MAITRE d': (*Returns smile.*) Right this way Miss. (*Seats her at a small table for two.*) A waiter will be right with you Miss.
TERESA STEIN: Oh, I feel faint, oh I need something sweet ... I really want ... (*She faints, falling on the floor.*)
(*Pause*)
MAITRE d': (*Runs over and bends down, then spies a waiter.*) Call nine-one-one Jose, **NOW!"**

SCENE 2

Setting: Long General hospital room

TERRY McCALLUM: (*Addressing a woman she believes to be a doctor.*) Is this the one who needs his respirator shut off Doctor?
JUDY COLLINS: (*Frowns and shakes her head.*) Yes, it is nurse and my name is Judy Collins and I am a respiratory therapist.
TERRY McCALLUM: Oh, yes, of course Judy and I'm Terry. (*Offers hand and they shake.*)
JUDY COLLINS: (*Hands her a clipboard.*) Nice to meet you Terry but

I have to get back to intensive care. His name is James Higgins, Terry, first one on the top. Bye now and have a good shift.

TERRY McCALLUM: (*Watches Judy leave the room.*) Oh, well thank you very much. Bye now.

(*She walks to the beds and sees the name James Higgins and shuts off the ventilator and James Higgins, suffering from severe emphysema, quickly lapses into cardiac arrest. She walks out of the ward and an orderly quickly accosts her.*)

ORDERLY: Say nurse, a patient in six-oh-one needs an RN.

TERRY McCALLUM: (*Enters the room, just adjacent where they stood*) Hello, do you need a nurse?

TERESA STEIN: (*Hands her a prescription.*) Could you please get this re-filled? My doctor's name is on the front there, Sam Berger, it's Nardil. (*Beat*)

TERRY McCALLUM: (*Smiles.*) Oh, that's the brand name it's actually Phenelzine—I'll fill it for you Miss Stein in a minute.

TERESA STEIN (*Smiles.*) Oh, thank you so much nurse. (*Light fades.*)

SCENE 3

Setting: Hospital Pharmacy.

LINDA BLACK: (*Puts 4-dozen pills of Phenelzine in the container, hands it to the nurse and then smiles at the next nurse in line.*) Can I help you?

NURSE: Oh, oh, can you fill this prescription please?"
(*Pause*)

LINDA BLACK: (*Turns to audience and smiles.*) Oh, I love filling prescriptions, it's so easy. (*hums and sings while she puts pills in bottles.*) Two dozen of Peneeel Sulfat (*Phenelzine Sulfate*) in this little

bottle and now ... wait this is not Peneeel Sulfat it's Perpeenzeen, hee-heee, crazy name boy (*Perphenazine*). Well, I'll just put these in here and then this one here in here too also I'll hmmm-hmmm, oh, so much fun. (*She mixes the pills together without realizing it and even puts some Phenobarbital in the same container, jabbering away as she slips the pills, that would easily kill the sixty-seven-year-old patient within hours of mixing them, into the container.*)
LINDA BLACK: (*Smiles at the next customer.*) Oh, hi Terry.|
(*Beat.*)
TERRY McCOLLUM: (*Hands her the prescription.*) Hi Linda, could you fill this please?
(*Beat*)
LINDA BLACK: (*Turns to audience and give a sardonic, beastly smile.*) Oh, of course I can, I just *love* this job so much, it's soooo easy, oh yes. Hmmm-hummmm. (*Puts pills into various bottles while she is speaking.*)

SCENE 4

Setting: Teresa Stein's hospital room.

TERESA STEIN: (*Takes plastic pill container from Terry McCollum and immediately pops one into her mouth, swallowing a glass of water.*) Oh, thank you so much nurse.
Dr. PETER PAULSON: (*Strolls into the room.*) Well, what seems to be the problem? I'm Doctor Paulsen, by the way.
(*Beat.*)
TERESA STEIN: Oh, well, I passed out this afternoon, in a restaurant. I, that is, I really feel bad but well, I have this pain in my head and sometimes ...

Dr. PETER PAULSON: (*Waves his hand in the air, as if at a troublesome fly.*) I know *exactly* what you need, give her some Demerol nurse.
(*Beat*)
TERESA STEIN: No, Doctor, I think I need to see my physician first, Doctor Berger, Sam Berger, he's in Coral Springs?"
Dr. PETER PAULSON: Why, whatever for, dear girl? It's two in the morning?
TERESA STEIN: Oh? It is? Well, I'm taking Nardil you know?
TERRY McCALLUM: (*Superior smile.*) Phenelzine, Doctor.
Dr. PETER PAULSON: Well, I just want to help your pain, young lady, alright? Meperidine, ah Demerol, will do you some good—okay?
(*Beat*)
TERESA STEIN: Well, if you say so, Doctor?
Dr. PETER PAULSON: (*Smiles, even superior to the nurse's.*) I do.
(*Beat*)
TERRY McCALLUM: (*Takes the prescrition that Paulson has just scribbled on a prescription pad.*) Thank you Dr. Paulsen, I'll go fill this immediately.

BLACKOUT
(CURTAIN)

REQUIEM

Setting: Long General Hospital. When curtain rises we see several scenes in progress, where the patients will not make it. And, then a
VOICE: Yes, Long General is on a roll this humid, starry, South Florida evening and will go on to roll up a human death toll of thirteen human beings, a baker's dozen. Besides James Higgins, who is mistaken for Jerome Higgins, another patient, who died within an hour of his respirator being shut off there was Teresa Stein, who will die within two hours of taking Meperidine Hydrochloride, or Demerol that Paulson had prescribed for her, for when taken with the Nardil, it was potent enough to kill an average male, much less a frail female, as it would do, to her in the early morning hours of February but Paulsen wasn't finished; he was on a roll, having just come from surgically removing 69-year-old Tim Wades' right leg. Actually, it hadn't been as bad as it could have been, considering Paulsen's lack of training and without the assistance of a first-year intern it certainly could have caused Wades' death, which might have served Wade better, considering he still had his diseased left leg, as Paulsen had amputated the wrong one. Dr. Stanley Crushhorn, an alcoholic anesthesiologist, who had had his license to practice medicine pulled in three states but, nevertheless was legally practicing at Long General, and was ably assisted by Gina Zerba, one of We Care's imposter's, administers enough anesthesia to kill the man ten times over, but, of course, once is enough, and it seems then, that not only Paulsen is on a roll but that Long General Hospital is on a roll, a roll that will vacate some much-needed patient suites: patient suites that will be filled the same day that they become available by, of course, some *really sick* people. Besides Teresa Stein, Linda Black would poison three other patients by mixing prescription drugs together and those, along with the

patient that Dr. Stanley Crushhorn, with the help of Gina Zerba, will anesthetize to death, seven more unlucky humans will meet their deaths, three at the hands of the imposter Dr. Peter Paulsen and four at the hands of various and assorted other imposters, some who would be caught and fined or imprisoned and some who would escape totally unscathed. There will be lawsuits, recriminations, back-stabbings and finger-pointing ad infinitum but nothing will really change, as the system will continue unabated, feeding off itself, when the temp agencies, insurance adjusters and hospital administrators attack and tear at each other, becoming pitiful, primitive caricatures of the human race, as they are pitted against each other by the human sharks that are more commonly known as lawyers, who will pit employee against employee, each one blaming the other, as bankruptcy filings are bandied about and the sharks at the top of the food chain, the lawyers, keep the rivalries alive, lining their pockets with more and more gold, as they swim around in the ocean, also known as a courtroom, biting and tearing at each other, on behalf of their clients and the system that they have helped to create and flourish under them, as long as they can legally continue to capitalize on the rules, the laws, many of which they themselves have made, to beg, bargain and steal to their gain: their quite profitable gain.

BIG SUGAR
AN ORIGINAL PLAY IN 3 ACTS & A REQUIEM

CHARACTERS:

THOMAS WANG: Owns computer tech company. Age 30.
HISPANIC MAN aka FLASH: Age 30-40.
MOSES MOORE aka BIG SUGAR: Jamaican, 6'4", 250 lbs. Age 33.
PORT AUTHORITY POLICEMAN (unnamed.) Age 30-40.
JIMMY PORELLI: Transit Authority Policeman, Age 41.
BLACKSNAKE: Homeless man, Age 30-40.
2 HOMOSEXUALS IN BATHROOM STALL: Ages 20-40
4 CRACK-ADDICTS: Ages 20-45.
LT. FELIX BANDORA aka THE CAT: Port Authority cop. Age 35-45
PAUL MASON aka WHEELCHAIR PAUL: Homeless, Age 35.
BILLY: Port Authority policeman. Age 30-40.
ROSE: Homeless, amputee prostitute. Age 45-55
DUMB EDDIE: Retarded 18 year-old man, thinks Doris is his mother.
DORIS: 20-year-old homeless girl
FATHER JAMES J. HENNESY: Priest. Age 60.
JOE MARABELLI: Ex-champion fighter now homeless. Age 50-60.
MICKEY McLARNIN: Transit Authority Policeman, Age 30-40.

ACT I
3 SCENES

We see into the Port Authority Bus Station, in Manhattan, New York City and it's residents, those homeless who live there and those, like the police and world travelers who they deal with, daily.

ACT I   SCENES & SETTINGS

SCENE 1: Setting: Port Authority Bus Terminal
SCENE 2: Setting: Men's bathroom
SCENE 3: Police Station

ACT II
2 SCENES

The basement is a netherworld of homeless, drug-addicted, residents who have been written off by the world and deal daily only with the police and others who live in their world of poverty and hopelessness and who have no fear of the police but only of losing their high(s).

ACT II   SCENES & SETTINGS

SCENE 1: Setting: Port Authority Basement
SCENE 2: Setting: Police Station

ACT III
3 SCENES

We see into the worst of the basement purgatory and a Savior named Big Sugar, who rescues those no one else can.

ACT III   SCENES & SETTINGS

SCENE 1: Setting: Emergency stairwells
SCENE 2: Setting: Terminal entrance on 42nd St. and Eighth Ave.
SCENE 3: Setting: Alleyway by St. Patrick's Cathedral

REQUIEM
Setting: Church

ACT I
SCENE 1

Setting: Port Authority Bus Terminal, New York City.

(*As curtain opens, we see Thomas Wang inside the Port Authority Bus Terminal, at the North entrance on the corners of 42nd Street and Eighth Avenue. Wang is the CEO of Wang International, a huge computer-tech firm, and he is in a hurry. Wang has, for the first time in his life, used the mass transit system, his limo driver is ill, and he decides to take the bus back to his palatial estate in New Jersey, even though several of his staff minions have offered to drive him but Wang has been offered a large block of shares in a bus company, as part of a microchip computer deal and wants to see firsthand just exactly what he might be getting involved in. He has to go to the bathroom and spies a men's room but also a public phone and he has left his cellphone, unknown by most residents in 1989, in his limo. Just as he takes the telephone off the receiver, a Hispanic man wearing an orange wool-knit cap that was pulled down over his forehead eyes him warily and nudges his arm.*)

HISPANIC MAN aka FLASH: Hey-yah got a numbah for youse mane.
THOMAS WANG: Excuse me?
FLASH: Mane, I got a card numbah for yah mane. Yah can call anywhere in ah world for free mane, gimme a nickel for it mane. C'mon you can call China all night mane, ees good.
WANG: Excuse me but I have my own credit cards if I need to call anyone, anywhere. I left my cell-phone in my limo.
FLASH: Shell-phone? Was-ah dat mane, sumteeng for Shell gas? Hey, c'mon gimme a fin for dees mane; I gots a round ah bread waitin' on me, gimme a nickel mane, I needs dat vial bad mane, c'mon now! Eees numbah ees good. (*He grabs Wang by the shirt and they begin scuffling,*

until the drug-addicted thug is picked up bodily, from behind, and thrown to the floor.)
BIG SUGAR: (*Jamaican, 6'4" and 250 lbs. He addresses the Hispanic man by his street name.*) Git on Flash and leave this mahn alone.
FLASH: Ah-nah, I wuz jus' ask-in' diz mane here for some money is all Big Sugar, youse know? Okay beeg mane, ees all good, ees … (*Runs away. He was a champion sprinter in high school and almost bowls over a policeman on his sprint away from Big Sugar.*)
JIMMY PORELLI: (*Transit Authority Policeman, walks over to Big Sugar and Thomas Wang.*) Say Big Sugar, what's goin' on here anyway, man? I saw Flash over here, is he high again?
WANG: Officer that man was assaulting me for money, he wanted to sell me some sort of card number and this man came over as we were wrestling on the floor and he saved my life; he saved my life I tell you.
POLICEMAN: (*He has heard this same tribute from many grateful commuters, as well as homeless beggars and itinerants, all of whom had been rescued by the big Jamaican, from someone attempting to do them harm.*) Good job Big guy, we appreciate it.
WANG: Oh-ah-er, I have to use the bathroom, if …
JIMMY PORELLI: Oh just over there sir. (*Points at the men's room sign. Jimmy Porelli, a New York City policeman for nearly 22 years and with the transit authority for the last 7, has just turned 41. Porelli is thankful for the big Jamaican's presence, as the Port Authority police can use all the help they can get. He sees a young Hispanic boy eyeballing an elderly woman and then watches as the boy snatches her purse and takes off running. Looks at Big Sugar.*) I'll get him, t'anks again fer the help Big Guy. (*Runs after purse-snatcher.*)
WANG: (*Big Sugar disappears and Wang decides that after he uses the bathroom he will call a limousine service.*) Now, where did that big guy get to? I wanted to give him some money? Damn it. (*Walks towards bathroom and light fades on this side of the stage as Wang enters bathroom and comes up on the other side where we see Big Sugar talking to Stella, a one-legged diabetic, who lived in a wheelchair and*

makes her living begging coins in the Port Authority bus station.)
BIG SUGAR: What happened Stell'?
STELLA: It were Blacksnake Sugah, he, he gots all my beggings money, my dinnah money too Sue-gar, six bucks.
BIG SUGAR: Oh, that's tur-bull Stella, that's ... (*Big Sugar sees the culprit himself standing several yards away staring intently at Stella and Big Sugar knew immediately that Blacksnake realized that the jig was up when he smiles deceptively and then turns and runs for cover. It is shoulder to shoulder on 42nd Street at this hour, just after 8:00 PM, and Blacksnake, who knew every crack and crevice in the sidewalks, soon disappears from view.*)
BIG SUGAR: (*Walks back into the Port Authority where innumerable drug-addicts and alcoholics as well as the mentally ill, the incapable and the infirm, and those innumerable human beings that found themselves homeless through circumstance, a stroke of bad luck or just that cruel, miscalculating master of us all, fate, found themselves. The Port was a veritable glass and steel-girded city within a city, for most of them. The sprawl of the two lengthy city-blocks, located in the heart of downtown Manhattan, provides this ragamuffin population with enough unguarded tourists and unsuspecting travelers for many of them to virtually make their living's off the marks, robbing and stealing from them indiscriminately, and using most of their booty to buy drugs or alcohol from the numerous dealers in and around the Port and they all knew Big Sugar's story, that he had come up from Belle Glade, in Florida, where he had been working, cutting sugar cane and, as the story went, had come to New York after injuring, or even killing, one of the bosses who worked for one of the major sugar cartels, cartels that held enormous financial as well as political power in the State of Florida.*) Stella, he gone, I couldn't catch him but I will get him and your money soon enough, okay?
STELLA: I knows you will Sue-gar, I knows it, if on-nee I had me sumpin' to eat?
BIG SUGAR: (*Pulls out a sandwich from his coat-pocket.*) Here you go

Stell', Father Hennessy gave it to me earlier, it's yours.
STELLA: (*Taking the sandwich.*) But, you needs to eat too Sue-gar, you should eat diz sam'ich?
(*Beat*)
BIG SUGAR: I ate enough today, eat it Stella, you need it more than than I do.
(*Beat*)
STELLA: Oh thank you Sue-gar, thanks you so much. (*Bites into sandwich*) You ste-ill gots yo' knife Sue-gar?
BIG SUGAR: (*Dressed in faded blue-jeans, a woolen shirt that helped to camouflage a razor-sharp thirty-inch long machete and a pair of fifteen triple E work boots that he had purchased for a cut-rate price at a downtown Army-Navy store.*) I have it Stella, stop worryin'.
STELLA: You know Sue-gar, 'snake take advantage ah me now allah time because he t'ink I still his ho' and he …
BIG SUGAR: Do not worry about that Stellah, I will watch out for him.
STELLA: I knows you will, I be safe now that chew-is here now.
(*Beat*)
BIG SUGAR: (*Smiles showing several gold-capped teeth and a pressing need of further dental work.*) Stop worrying and everything will be alright.
(*Beat*)
STELLA: (*A man drops a dollar bill in her cup and she smiles up at Big Sugar.*) Yes, I know I will, now that you're back near me Sue-gar.
BIG SUGAR: (*Is considered a savior by many, like Stella, and a nightmare for others, like Blacksnake, who would stay away from the Port for many weeks to come, his fear of Big Sugar enough to do what no blue uniform and badge had ever done.*) I'm here with you Stella, just don't worry no more.
(*Beat*)
STELLA: (*Smiles when a man drops a fifty-cent piece in her tin cup.*) I ain't gone worry now you is here; you is my savior.

SCENE 2

Setting: Men's bathroom. *(Inside the 'Men' bathroom on the second floor, two transvestites are engaging in an immoral act behind a closed and locked stall door, their growling and moaning being totally ignored by the four drug addicts who sat in a corner taking turns passing around a crack pipe. One of the addicts, a transvestite with a two-day-old beard showing through his pancake make-up and totally oblivious of the perverted rumblings inside the room, nevertheless, looks up startled when Thomas Wang opens the door and walks into the rank public restroom. The transvestite's staring demeanor alerts the other junkies and they all look up and see a mark, a mark wearing an Armani suit that they all envisioned was filled with cash, cash that they could buy more crack with, a habit they all shared and would do anything to feed.)*
WANG: *(Hurries to urinal and unzips his fly, where the transvestite brushes up against him.)* Sorry, I didn't see you there.
TRANSVESTITE ADDICT: Oooohhh honey, I'll do youse fo' a quarter?
(Beat)
WANG: Please leave me alone sir. *(Suddenly, the door to the toilet where the two homosexuals had been opens and they run out of the stall and out of the bathroom door, even as one of the four crack-heads jumps on Wang's back and pulls him down to the cold, hard tile floor. He's wrestling with Wang when another crack addict reaches for Wang's coat pocket and a stream of Wang's urine smacks him in the face, streaming down into his nostrils and mouth.)*
(Beat)
CRACK ADDICT: Ah-ehah, piss on me mahn, muhfuh I'll fuminin' kill you—I'll kill you! *(The addict pulls out a roofer's knife and the others begin kicking and beating on him: his screams are easily heard. Scene darkens and then lightens upon Big Sugar, walking when he spies a friend, Wheelchair Paul, who is trying to open the bathroom door.*

Light comes up outside the bathroom.)
BIG SUGAR: (*Walks to where Wheelchair Paul is struggling to open the bathroom door.*) Paul, mahn, what are yah doing mahn?
(*Beat*)
WHEELCHAIR PAUL: Ah, Big Sugar, my friend, I can't seem to get this door open.
BIG SUGAR: Here, my good friend, I will help you. (*Big Sugar puts his hand on the door handle and, as he does, it flies open and slams against his steel wheelchair—shoving him backwards against the tiled wall—as all pandemonium breaks loose when his chair rolls backwards towards the entrance of the bathroom, partially blocking it, as four crack-heads pile through the opening all at once. One of the crack-heads shoves the wheelchair aside and comes face to face with Big Sugar. A Rastafarian, from the same West Indies Island as Big Sugar, the crack-head knows him only by his street name and legendary unrivaled reputation for protecting the weak and helpless, even unto risking his own life and limb, he was known for being absolutely fearless, remarkably strong, and capable of superhuman feats of strength, that had cowed even the bravest and most reckless of thugs.*)
CRACKHEAD: (*Eyes magnify and a look of fear comes upon his face.*) Ah mahn—Big Sugar?
(*Beat*)
 BIG SUGAR: Git on niggah. (*All four crack-heads quickly storm past Big Sugar and run, stumbling down the stairs, toward the nearest exit in the Port's main concourse.*)
WHEELCHAIR PAUL: Oh man, Big man, those guys scared ah youse fah sure.
(*Beat*)
BIG SUGAR: You have to use the bathroom?
WHEELCHAIR PAUL: Boy, I'll say, if I can ever get inside to relieve my bladder. Hey, you look hungry; here I gotta half a sandwich."
BIG SUGAR: (*Pushes the sandwich back into Wheelchair Paul's shirt.*) Don't want yo' sam-itch Paulie—c'mon let's get you inside. (*Opens

door and nods at Wheelchair Paul, who, he knows, insists on doing everything himself.*) Well? Roll on inside, Paulie.
WHEELCHAIR PAUL: (*Grabs his wheels but stops up short.*) Gee-zuz Mary and Joseph, will yah lookit this Big Guy?
(*Beat*)
BIG SUGAR: (*Steps into the bathroom and stops next to the immobile wheelchair, staring at the bloody carnage that is lying in a heap in the middle of the floor. It had once been a man but his face was a mass of unrecognizable flesh, with blood-streaked facial bones and teeth scattered at intervals just adjacent to the corpse. The man's clothes are soaked in blood and strewn in shredded strips across the tile floor. Big Sugar walks closer and stares at the lumpy mass that had once been a human being's face. He peers closer and closer, as if it is a rattlesnake poised to strike and Wheelchair Paul's eyes mimicked Big Sugar's, gazing hypnotically at the slimy corpse. Then, they both see it, at the same instant, and both men recoil at the sight. Big Sugar exhales audibly and spits on the floor.*) Animals, they are animals who did this mahn, they are not human beings.
WHEELCHAIR PAUL: (*Rolls his wheelchair to within a few feet of Wang's body.*) Oh my Gawd, Big Sugar, they cut off his pecker and ... Gee-zuz Gawd help them.
(*Beat*)
BIG SUGAR: Yah mahn, I see they stuffed it in his mouth. They are not human beings. (*Big Sugar sees the man's suit, although bloodied, was an expensive one with the initials T.W. on cuff-linked shirtsleeves and suddenly a bell went off inside his head, as he remembers the oriental man that he had rescued earlier that evening, from another addict. He was certain that this was the same man and his hand balled up, into a massive fist.*)
(*Beat*)
WHEELCHAIR PAUL: (*Sees Big Sugar's anger.*) Big Sugar, we better report this, the police station's just aroun' ah corner.
BIG SUGAR: (*Smiles at the irony of this fact.*) No Paulie, I am going

after the killers mahn, I know who they are; you can go report it. You know as well as I do that the po-leece nevah do nuttin' anyway, mahn?
WHEELCHAIR PAUL: (*His eyes flick to the corpse and then back to Big Sugar.*) "I know it Big Man but I think they will *this time!*"
BIG SUGAR: (*His eyes flash back to the corpse.*) What do you mean mahn? Why would they?
WHEELCHAIR PAUL: Look at this man's demeanor and dress, he is a mover and shaker. He's a man of wealth and power and the police are as political an organization as any other and all the killings at the Port Authority are almost always street people killing other street people, which to the police is just one less lowlife but let a wealthy man be murdered and the politicians, who are also wealthy men themselves, will come out crying law and order.
BIG SUGAR: You are a very smart mahn Paulie but when did you see this man before coming into this bathroom?
(*Beat*)
WHEELCHAIR PAUL: I saw him talking to you by the pay-phone but I was eating and too many around me were begging me to give them some and I couldn't concentrate but I could see him and heard what he said to Flash.
(*Beat*)
BIG SUGAR: (*Smiles at Wheelchair Paul, showing several gold-capped teeth.*) Yah mahn, you are very observant mahn, very smart. You should have finished your studies. Oh, sorry mahn.
(*Beat*)
WHEELCHAIR PAUL: (*Had been a year shy of getting a science degree when his parents died and the money stopped and Wheelchair Paul hated to even think of that time, much less talk about it.*) It's alright big guy, you are a Savior, everybody here knows it too. We know you are closer to God than we are because we have seen it but we must report this to the police now or we'll be in big trouble, you know?
BIG SUGAR: I feel my power comes from above Paulie and we both know that every life is equal but I think that this man has a family and

now that family will be deprived of him. But, Paulie, this vicious of a deed will hurt all of us; all the homeless and helpless in the Port because the police will now see the corpse, and blame us, the poor and homeless. They will now make a deadly sweep of the area. (*Nods at Wheelchair Paul and then at the door*) Paulie, let's go and see the po-leece, mahn."
WHEELCHAIR PAUL: Now you're talkin' Big Sugar, let's go. (*Beat*)
BIG SUGAR: (*As they make their way towards the police station, Big Sugar sees that it's hopeless and the clock is ticking; he could see that the cells were jam-packed, as were the wall shackles. He knew that every second that went by made it that much harder for him to catch up with the merciless quartet of murderous crack addicts. He grabs Wheelchair Paul's arm.*) Paulie, make a report mahn. I am going after these wolves for they have caught the scent of blood and may do more mayhem. They are looking for a few rounds of bread and will stop at nothing to get it. I mean to find them mahn; make the report and show the po-leece the dead mahn's body.
WHEELCHAIR PAUL: Will do Big guy, be careful Big Sugar and may God be with you. (*Sighs, then nods even as Big Sugar is gone, his huge form disappearing into the thick crowd of bodies, almost like a ghost.*)

SCENE 3

Setting: Port Authority Police Station.

LT. FELIX BANDORA aka THE CAT: (*Scowls at Wheelchair Paul.*) Yeah, what was that again? I din' catch youse drift sport, yah sumpin' about the bad'room ah sumpin'?
WHEELCHAIR PAUL: Well, I was wonderin' sir, if you could come and look inside the men's bathroom because …

LT. BANDORA: Lis'sen I got a hun'erd men all over dah Port right now and we got none to spare, look-it dah cells, look-it dah day-yum wall shackles, huh? Yeah, yeah (*sees Wheelchair Paul looking at the wall-shackled prisoners and those practically back to back in the cells available*) Yeah, we can't transfer 'em to the station houses fast enough. So, no I can't and nor can any of my men go and look in dah damn men's room. Unless (*Bandora sarcastically mocks Wheelchair Paul*) you perhaps have a dead body in there? (*Turns his attention to a stack of police reports and arrests in front of him and barely hears Wheelchair Paul's answer.*)
(*Beat*)
WHEELCHAIR PAUL: Ah, yessir, we, do have that, that is …
LT. BANDORA: What? Did you say sumpin' dere *again* sport?
(*Beat*)
WHEELCHAIR PAUL: Ah, yes, yessir, there is a dead body in the men's room, sir.
(*Pause*)
LT. BANDORA: (*Stares menacingly at Wheelchair Paul.*) Let me get this straight sport, you gotta dead body in the men's bad'room?
(*Beat*)
WHEELCHAIR PAUL: Yessir, there is … a dead body … in the men's bathroom, sir.
(*Beat*)
LT. BANDORA: (*Glares at Wheelchair Paul menacingly, yet again, then glances around the room and finally spots a free cop.*) Jimmy, Jimmy, c'mere a sec'.
(*Beat*)
JIMMY PORELLI: (*Shakes his head resignedly: he had been busy and had just that very second finished a report on a burglary but knew better than to feign being too busy to report to the watch commander.*) Yeah, L-Tee, wah'sup?
LT. BANDORA: Jimmy diz is, ah-ner-um-ah, what's yah name sport? (*Looks down at Wheelchair Paul*)

(*Beat*)
WHEELCHAIR PAUL: Paul sir, Paul Mason.
(*Beat*)
LT. BANDORA: (*Turns towards Officer Jimmy Porelli.*) Ah, Jimmy, Paul Mason here says there is a dead body in the men's room. Isn't that correct there Mr. Mason?
(*Beat*)
WHEELCHAIR PAUL: Ah, ah, yessir, it is correct?
(*Beat*)
LT. BANDORA: (*Rolls his eyes at Porelli*) Check it out will yah Jimmy? (*Turns to another Port Authority cop*) Billy, 'id youse get those Knicks tickets for me?
(*Beat*)
COP: (*Reaches into his coat pocket and come out with two tickets to the Knicks game. Hands them to Bandora*) Here yah go Skipper, hey what was dat? (*Watches Porelli walk out with Wheelchair Paul.*) What's all that about Skipper?
LT. BANDORA: Eh, the crip' says there's a stiff in the terlet.
COP: Yeah, garbage on garbage Skip—all we ever get anymore.
LT. BANDORA: Yeah, maybe a wino passed out there or sumpin' yah know Bill?
(*Beat*)
JIMMY PORELLI: (*Looks at Wheelchair Paul and then at Bandora, who is already occupied talking to another one of his cops.*) Okay, champ, let's go. Lead the way, lead the way.
(*Beat*)
WHEELCHAIR PAUL: Yes sir, it's just over here.
JIMMY PORELLI: (*Walking beside the wheelchair.*) Okay, we're there. I'll go in first. (*Holding the door open for Wheelchair Paul, Porelli immediately spies the dead body.*)

CURTAIN
INTERMISSION

ACT II
SCENE 1

Setting: When curtain rises we see Port Authority's basement, a netherworld of intransigence and insanity known only to the homeless residents who live there and the police that swept the area regularly.

BIG SUGAR: (*When the curtain rises we see Big Sugar going into the Port's basement. He passes several junkies, all passing a crack pipe around and stops just beside them.*) Seen anyone running this way?
(*Beat*)
JUNKIE: (*Holds crack pipe out to Big Sugar.*) Wanna hit bro-ah?
(*Beat*)
BIG SUGAR: (*Waves this gesture away.*) No mahn. (*Sees they're all too high to help and moves down further into the basement.*)
(*Beat*)
TRANSVESTITE: (*Standing against a wall, pulls up his shirt, revealing a flabby breast.*) Want some titty baby—huh?
BIG SUGAR: (*Scowls and shakes his head, disgust obvious on his face, then is drawn towards a commotion coming from the end of a narrow curving pathway, where we see a darkened corner begin lighting up. We see an old blanket hanging from a water pipe, partially covering a chair. Big Sugar moves in for a closer inspection, even as we hear someone moaning and the chair creaking. We hear a man's voice bark something unintelligible and then the blanket parts and a form appears and walks past Big Sugar. He smiles at Big Sugar.*) Cheap head man. (*At the same instant we hear a woman's voice.*) Hey-hey, come back here youse bastid, youse ain't paid me yet.
BIG SUGAR: (*Walks to the blanket being used as a curtain, and moves it aside. Sitting in a wheelchair we see an old woman, who only stops*

screaming when she sees Big Sugar.) Rose, what are you doing? You need to stop these evil ways?
(*Beat*)
ROSE: Big Sue-gar, stop dat man, he raped me Big Sue .. he …
(*Beat*)
BIG SUGAR: (*We see Big Sugar scowl at the woman: she is a notorious prostitute known for screaming rape whenever any of her Johns fails to pay her, which, in the Port's own personal Purgatory, was more often than not. We see Rose, known vicariously as Fat Rose, grab a beer bottle and take a quick gulp from it. She has one leg amputated at the knee and an eye-patch over one eye.*) Listen to me now Rose, you must stop this way of living. I will move you upstairs, remember how you and Stella watched out for each other? She's still up there you know?
(*Beat*)
ROSE: Dey robs her too Big Sue-gar, I knows, I knows she jes' got robbed; I know, Blacksnake he come runnin' down here blabbin' his mouf off and I heared 'em, dey was all runnin' and dey ...
BIG SUGAR: Blacksnake? You seen Blacksnake Rose, where he be?
ROSE: I ain't Big Sue-gar, really I ain't he jes' was braggin' to some drag queens about how he …
BIG SUGAR: Drag Queens. Listen to me closely now Rose. I am looking for four men, two are black, two are white. One that I know is the leader and his name is Ramon Paul and he is Jamaican, like me, he is very big almost as tall as I am but also very skinny, they are all crack addicts and they have killed a man in a horrible way, you understand what I'm sayin' Rose?
ROSE: (*We can tell that she stops listening when she realizes it doesn't benefit her personally.*) I hear you Big Sue-gar.
(*Beat*)
BIG SUGAR: Well, did you see him?
ROSE: Go get dat man Big Sue-gar, he take my cig'rettes.
(*Beat*)

BIG SUGAR: (*Realizes it's hopeless to talk to her but puts his face next to hers and speaks menacingly.*) Rose, have you seen Ramon Paul?
ROSE: He hurt me Big Sugar?
BIG SUGAR: He won't I promise you Rose, I will protect you from them all; you know I will?
(*Beat*)
ROSE: I knows you will Big Sue-gar, I knows it, you is so good, you is my Savior, you is my (*begins crying and grabs Big Sugar, who hugs her tightly, as she cries loudly.*) I see him, Big Sue-gar, I see him and the other preverts; they runnin' fast and one call himself Suzie, he fall down and he was bleedin' from his head and he seen me and said to say nuffin' when cops ask me about dem? I scared Big Sue-gar dose is preverts?
BIG SUGAR: You know any more of their names?
(*Beat*)
ROSE: No, jus' dat one you say, call hisse'f Ray-mone Paul and dat Suzie, he is white and gots red hair like dyed all red and he is ugly, he gots scars all over him. His arms and all, they is evil, dey will hoit me Big Sue-gar.
(*Beat*)
BIG SUGAR: No, they won't, you'll be aw'ight. I must go get them now. Try to mend your ways woman.
(*Beat*)
ROSE: I ain't 'fraid no mo' now you'is here. You my Savior Big Sue-gar.
(*Beat*)
BIG SUGAR: I will see you sometime soon, okay? Stop misbehaving and go upstairs with Stella. If you are still here when I come back I will take you up there myself, understand wha' I mean woman?
(*Beat*)
ROSE: I do it Big Sue-gar, I goin' up dere right away. (*She starts gathering up her junk and Big Sugar smiles and quickly departs. We see him running down the winding, concrete netherworld of the Port Authority Bus Terminal, as the light fades away.*)

SCENE 2

Setting: Police Station. (*As the curtain opens we see Captain Joseph Giambra reading a report. He is sitting at his desk and we see two policemen sitting in chairs adjacent to this desk. We recognize them as being Lt. Felix Bandora and Officer Jimmy Porelli.*)

CAPT. GIAMBRA: Youse guys are tellin' me diz guy had is peckah cut off and stuck in 'is mouth?
(*Beat*)
OFFICER PORELLI: I ain't seen nothin' like it since 'Nam Skipper.
CAPT. GIAMBRA: What ah youse t'ink Cat—a hit?
(*Beat*)
LT. BANDORA: Yeah, could be. I mean we need to eye-dee the body and see whether it's a wiseguy or what AND C.S.I., is over there now, so we're probably lookin' at more'n a few hours. I mean this guy did obviously have a set of expensive threads on and he had no wallet or jewelry, picked 'im clean.
CAPT. GIAMBRA: Yeah, they coulda done it jus' to make it look like a robbery. I t'ink we should sweep the place, wha' ah youse t'ink Cat?
(*Beat*)
LT. BANDORA: (*Glances outside the door, to where Wheelchair Paul sat in an otherwise isolated corner.*) Well Joe, I dunno, this guy in ah chair says diz jah-mook frien' ah his is on ah trail right now and he means to find them and extract some payback.
(*Pause*)
CAPT. GIAMBRA: (Follows Bandora's gaze to Wheelchair Paul and then eyes Porelli.) What yah say Jimmy?
OFFICER PORELLI: Sir, I know this man, this Jamaican, and I t'ink he'll do what he says he'll do. Big Sugar's a pretty capable guy, Skipper.

(*Beat*)
CAPT. GIAMBRA: (*Lights a cigarette, then eyeballs Porelli and Bandora.*) Big Sugar? Streetname?
OFFICER PORELLI: Yes sir, he protects the homeless people around the Port sir; I mean, that is, he has before and he does help us a lot.
(*Beat*)
CAPT. GIAMBRA: (*Giambra has worked his way up the chain of command and shows amusement at what Porelli has just said. He blows smoke-rings in the air.*) What ah youse mean Officer Porelli? Isn't this Jamaican homeless himself? Ain't diz the guy we put out an all-points on more'n once, din' he cut a guy's hand off a while back?
(*Beat*)
OFFICER PORELLI: (*Realizes that Giambra is being sarcastic when he calls him Officer Porelli. He's known Giambra for ten years and knows he doesn't pull rank but is making a point. Porelli smiles deceptively.*) They sewed the guy's hand back on: it was Card Mullins.
CAPT. GIAMBRA: Card Mullins, what, Card? Again?"
(*Beat*)
OFFICER PORELLI: Yes sir and he's already back on the street again but he hasn't worked the Port since.
CAPT. GIAMBRA: Card Mullins, why dat lowlife's been woikin' dah Port ever since I've had this command and that's six years in September, Geezuz, so *that's that* guy, he carries a Bowie knife ah sumpin'?
(*Beat*)
OFFICER PORELLI: A machete Skip'. (*Porelli's face takes on a puzzled look and then he shakes his fist.*) Skipper, I think I saw the deceased man earlier when I spoke to him about an incident with Flash, who was bothering this oriental man at a pay-phone. He asked me where the men's room was. Man, why didn't I remember this? Gee-zuz Skip it was this guy, I'm sure of it now that I think about it and Big Sugar had just saved the guy from Flash, who was tryin' to sell him something to get some more drugs. Same expensive suit. I'm sure of it now Cap'. And I think he probably went after these addicts and, like I said he's got this

machete and he knows how to use it?
(*Beat*)
CAPT. GIAMBRA: A machete …? What ah we got, a Crocodile Dundee chasin' around a bunch a crack-heads now or what?
(*Beat*)
OFFICER PORELLI: Well sir, Wheelchair Paul says that there were four transvestite crackheads and Big Sugar knew them so, like I say, he knows how quick these guys could disappear into the basements and, well, we'd never get them then. I mean, if he knows them? Well?
(*Beat*)
CAPT. GIAMBRA: Great, I gotta freakin' machete-wieldin' jah-mook chasin' a bunch a sissy he/she crack-heads all over dah Port. What a youse t'ink Jimmy? … Cat? We sweep the area?
(*Beat*)
OFFICER PORELLI: Cap' Big Sugar is a good man and he helps us quite a lot, we should look for him because if history holds true, Big Sugar will find these guys and then … well? (*Porelli looks over at Lt. Bandora.*)
(*Beat*)
LT. BANDORA: I think we gotta locate this molly-ah-nard Joe, I can roundup my best men, you know before we send the troops in, and see if we can find this Jamaican jahmook, this Big Sugar.
(*Beat*)
CAPT. GIAMBRA: Find this 'mook Cat. I give you 'till midnight.
(*Beat*)
LT. BANDORA: And what if we can't find him by then Cap'?
(*Beat*)
CAPT. GIAMBRA: We sweep!

CURTAIN

ACT III
SCENE 1

Setting: Emergency stairwells. (*As the curtain opens we see Big Sugar going through doors to the emergency stairwells. To the cops who sweep the Port Authority, the basement is considered to be purgatory; the stairwells are hell incarnate. Big Sugar sees small groups of men and women on every stair landing and the concrete floors are littered with crack vials, dead lighters, matchbooks, used condoms, dirty needles, belts, tubing and short pieces of rope.*)

BIG SUGAR: (*Hears his name called and looks up.*) Wha … ah …uht? Hey Eddie. (*A retarded man comes up to him. He is disheveled and homeless and Big Sugar has befriended him many times.*)
(*Beat*)
DUMB EDDIE: Big Shu-gah come wif me, Doris, gone kill 'ahse'f?
BIG SUGAR: Show me Eddie, show me where your mother is.
DUMB EDDIE: Come on I show you where she bees. (*Dumb Eddie slobbers on himself and starts walking downward. Light darkens as they walk to the other side of the stage. Light comes up on scene of an emergency stairwell where a woman is sitting on a battered, paint-splattered milk carton. She has a .44 caliber revolver in her right hand and is staring, glassy-eyed, at it. Big Sugar walks over to her.*)
BIG SUGAR: Hello Doris.
(*Pause*)
DORIS: (*Jerks her head up when she hears her name.*) Wha' … ah … uht? Who is that? (*She clutches a .44 caliber pistol closer to her bosom, pointing it inward, over her heart.*) No get away, I found it and it's mine. It can get rid of my constant pain. I know, I talked to it and it told me it would, I don't want no more bread; I wanna go home now. I wanna go

somewhere where there's no pain, the preacher tol' me there's no pain if I can just go home. (*Doris is a 22-year-old alcoholic who has become addicted to cocaine and has lived on the street for several years. She had befriended Dumb Eddie and he believed her to be the mother he had never known.*)
(*Beat*)
BIG SUGAR: Give me the gun Doris, give me the gun, you do not want to do this. What about your son Eddie? What will happen to him?
(*Beat*)
DORIS: (*Looks at Dumb Eddie.*) He not-dah, bummah my-nah-bup son, he a retard, he noump, I, I … (*Sticks the gun in her mouth and Big Sugar sees the motion and grabs the barrel. His grip is so powerful that by a mere twist of his wrist the gun-barrel quickly comes out of her mouth, slightly cutting the inside of her cheek. The pistol, a .44 Magnum, has been set to have a hair trigger and when Big Sugar pulls it from Doris' grasp it goes off, killing him instantly.*)
(*Pause*)
DUMB EDDIE: Oh-no-oooohhhhh. (l*ets out an inhuman, ghoulish howl that awakes even the most inebriated of the incoherent residents in this section of hell.*)
DORIS: No-no … no … (*It is also too much for Doris, who walks over to Big Sugar's corpse and snatches up the .44 Magnum, which is so full of blood and gristle that it nearly slips out of her hand but the hair-trigger outdoes even its own intentions when it goes off the instant that Doris turns it towards her own face, killing her instantly.*)

SCENE 2

Setting: North wing of Port authority Bus Station, corner of 42nd St. and Eighth Avenue.

WHEELCHAIR PAUL: (*Wheelchair Paul has known Stella for years but has never seen her in this state, she is no longer coherent. Wheelchair Paul has been hit hard also, by Big Sugar's death, but you had to go on living, eating and talking. The police have swept the area clean and most of the residents have spent a night or two in a jail-cell, as Wheelchair Paul had with Stella, but she had been totally mute then also. The police never found the four crack addicts who had murdered Thomas Wang but had thinned out the Port's homeless population almost in half, leaving only the physically and/or mentally ill such as Stella now seemed to qualify for, in both categories. She is emaciated to the extent that she looks like a skeleton. Wheelchair Paul touches her hand and she looks at him.*) Stella, it's all right, we can survive, please Stella, don't give up look, I have a ham sandwich; your favorite, from the Automat, fresh; it's fresh Stell', c'mon Stell', please, **PLEASE JESUS, PLEASE,** Stella.
(*Beat*)
STELLA: (*Looks at Wheelchair Paul but she is like a zombie, her eyes say nothing.*) All hope is gone, Big Sue-gah is dead, Paul, he is dead.

SCENE 3

Setting: A week later in an alleyway just past St. Patrick's Cathedral. (*It is 10:00 PM, on Christmas Eve and the bone-chilling cold makes Stella's teeth chatter, as her fingers turn numb. She hasn't eaten anything in over a week and is very weak and dehydrated, and her desire to live, which disappeared the moment she heard of Big Sugar's untimely death, has never been lower, as she mumbles incoherently, talking to herself and to what she perceived as God; she was looking for God and, being a lifelong Catholic, she knew exactly where to look; she had to get as close as she could to a church. As the night wears on and the bitter cold becomes even more unbearable, she hears the clanging of bells and suddenly realizes that it is midnight and that it is no longer Christmas Eve but Christmas Day. Her shrunken stomach trembles and she is suddenly awakened from her mental stupor and realizes that she is hungry, and remembers that Father Hennessy always visited the Port Authority on Christmas Day: he would transport anyone that would go, to a shelter for a traditional Christmas meal and shelter for the night and she quietly pondered attempting to steer her wheelchair back towards the Port Authority. Suddenly, she bows her head and prays with the last bit of her strength and we hear her praying.)*

STELLA: Oh, Lord I pray for Big Sugar's soul; I pray for my friends at the Port and I need you Lord, my heart and my soul have become lost, the people Lord, the people they, they are cold, they are heartless, Lord, the people, Lord Big Sue-gar, why did you have to take him from me, from us at the Port Authority Bus Term-nule? He was our Savior you see? Please Jesus, please, the pain is too much. (*She feels something pulling on her and opens her eyes and it was then that Big Sugar appears to her, once again. We see Big Sugar in the light, just as the light fades and the curtain drops.*)

REQUIEM

Setting: The front of a church where a priest, Father James J. Hennessy serves Christmas dinners to all the homeless who show up. (*Two priests, one of which is Father James J. Hennessy are standing in front of the church to meet the homeless who have been driven over on a bus that comes directly from the Port Authority Bus Terminal to the church. He always greets them, knowing most personally, as they enter the church while two other priests greet them as they get off the buses. He is* running late and sees two buses already parked and the homeless are departing.)

FATHER HENNESSY: Hey fellas, where's everybody at? Has anybody seen Stella? She's usually the first one here but ...
WHEELCHAIR PAUL: Geez, I dunno Faddah where Stella could be, but we're here and I sure am hungry.
ROSE: I'm really hungry too Faddah.
(*Beat*)
FATHER HENNESSY: (*Nods and holds open the door for both cripples, even though he knows they both disdain any such help, preferring to get along on their own steam. But, today, the holiest of days, they allow the priest the courtesy. Hennessy notices that several people are climbing off a bus that was parked just adjacent to the shelter. He frowns when he sees the number painted on its side, 500, as it is a bus that had been in the repair shop the last time he had seen it. He watches the transients head for the church and tells another priest he'll be right back. He walks to the 500 bus and opens the hood, where Hennessy sees that it is minus a water pump and the spark plugs are not even hooked up; it was indeed the defective bus that he had seen in the shop but who had towed it to the church? And why had they towed it to the church? Hennessy stares after some passengers, who had just stepped off the bus, and grabs the closest man, Gerald 'Hairy Jerry' Winslow a homeless man Hennessy knows has been living at the Port for the past year or so.*) Gerry, how are you? Did you just get off that bus?
HAIRY JERRY: Hey Faddah Hen-see, Mar-ree Criz-muz.
FATHER HENNESSY: Merry Christmas Gerry. Gerry, did you just get off that bus? Five-hundred is the number? Did you?
(*Beat*)
HAIRY JERRY: (*Glances at the bus with the number 500 on the side.*) Yeah Faddah, sure did. Big Shoe'gah drove us here in it.
(*Beat*)

FATHER HENNESSY: (*Sees a homeless woman he recognizes.*) Ah, Sue did you ...

DIRTY SUE: That's right Faddah, Big Sugar brought us, he loves us, he tol' me so.

(*Pause*)

FATHER HENNESSY: (*Turns pale because he knows Big Sugar has been killed in a gun accident. He had been the one to identify him by his given name Moses Moore.*) Has anyone else seen Big Sugar? (*Hennessy frowns and is stymied when several others, upon hearing the conversation, come over to confirm that Big Sugar, whom Hennessy well-knew had been killed in a gun accident, had brought them to the shelter, in the bus bearing the number 500. Hennessy pushes through the lengthening line and into the shelter and immediately sees Big Sugar, as he is standing talking to Eddie 'Dumb Eddie' Malone, a semi-retarded homeless man, who roamed the streets endlessly mumbling to himself. Next to Dumb Eddie was Wheelchair Paul, an epileptic cripple that Hennessy knew had an I.Q. that approached the genius range of two-hundred. Suddenly, Hennessy is grabbed by his forearm and spun around, by Joe 'Punchy Joe' Marabelli, an ex-prizefighter who had once been a world champion but now lived the life of an alcoholic, on the streets of the Bowery.*) What is it Joe?

(*Beat*)

JOE MARABELLI: Hey Faddah, Merry Criz-muz.

FATHER HENNESSY: (*Hennessy patted Punchy Joe's head, then quickly removed Joe's vice-like grip from his forearm. He approached Dumb Eddie and Wheelchair Paul but Big Sugar was gone.*) Eddie, who was that you were just talking to ... was it ...?

(*Beat*)

DUMB EDDIE: (*Bobs head up and down and swallows a mouthful of turkey.*) Yeah-up Faddah, 'at was Big Sugar. Yeah-up, he say Stella and Dora are happy now!

WHEELCHAIR PAUL: (*Smiles.*) Dumb Eddie's speaking the gospel Father that was Big Sugar and he said Stella and Doris are happy now.

(*Beat*)
FATHER HENNESSY: (*Recognizes two Port Authority cops, who are striding towards them. They were almost upon him, as he searched the room for Punchy Joe.*) What 'id Joe do this time?
(*Beat*)
OFFICER JIMMY PORELLI: Oh, it's not about Punchy this time Father. Look, Faddah, we know it's Christmas and all but we really need to ask for your help; we need an eye-dee?
(*Beat*)
FATHER HENNESSY: (*Hennessy frowns, no day is sacred in the city of New York, death is always ever present for him.*) Who was it Officer?
OFFICER MICKEY McLARNIN: It was One-legged Stella, you remember her, don't yah Faddah? She was here every Christmas for the past half-dozen years?
OFFICER JIMMY PORELLI: (*Shakes a cigarette from a crumpled-up pack and hands one to McLarnin when he motions for one.*) Yeah Father the one in the wheelchair, she was a diabetic, remember? You used to bring her insulin to the Port?
(*Beat*)
FATHER HENNESSY: What? You're kidding me aren't you?
(*Beat*)
OFFICER MICKEY McLARNIN: (*Exhales a stream of smoke and Father Hennessy bums one from Porelli.*) No Sir, one thing we never kid about is death, Father.
(*Beat*)
FATHER HENNESSY: (*His hand shakes as he lights the cigarette.*) What ah-er? How did she ah …?
(*Beat*)
OFFICER MICKEY McLARNIN: They found her body on Fifth Av-nah, next to Saint Patricks, on Fifth and fifty-fois' youse know?
(*Beat*)
FATHER HENNESSY: Yes-yes, I know it well. How did she ….
OFFICER MICKEY McLARNIN: Well sir, she officially froze to

death but foul play is suspected, know what I mean, ah, Faddah?
(*Beat*)
FATHER HENNESSY: Foul play Officer McLarnin?
(*Beat*)
OFFICER MICKEY McLARNIN: Well sir several witnesses saw her in an alleyway next to Saint Paddy's and also saw a big niggah, ah-er, I mean African-American, scuze me Faddah, ah diz African-American was seen hangin' aroun' her, see? So we figure he was probably robbin' her, know what I mean sir? The streets are bad sir, especially this time of the year; know what I mean Faddah?
(*Pause*)
FATHER HENNESSY: Wha … Sweet Jesus? (*Father James J. Hennessy immediately turns pale then jerks his head over towards where Dumb Eddie and Wheelchair Paul are both standing, grinning from ear-to-ear.*)

CURTAIN

END OF PLAY

THE SHEIK IS DEAD

A PLAY IN 3 ACTS

CHARACTERS:

GARY GREB: MAIN CHARACTER, REALTOR Age 35-45.
RALPH WILLIAMS: COMEDY CLUB M.C. Age 35-45
JAMES GAREN: MORTGAGE BROKER Age 40-50
STEVEN LATTNER-TITLE COMPANY OWNER Age 35-45
ELIZABETH ELKINS: REALTOR, Age 35-45
TERESA MANN: REALTOR, AGE 40
DIANE BRAMSON: GAREN'S SECRETARY, Age 25-30
JEFF BAKER: CLOSING AGENT AGE 35-45
DAVID REED: CAR SALESMAN Age 40
JACKIE BROWN: DISBARRED LAWYER, CAR SALESMAN Age 35-45
RECEPTIONIST Age 25-35
SECRETARY Age 25-35
BARTENDER Age 35-45
WAITER Age 20-30
SWARTHY MAN Age 30-40
SWARTHY ARAB Age 30-40
MAN ON ATLANTA FLIGHT Age 45-55
STEWARDESS Age 25-35
AIRPORT CROWD: (Can be actors or audience volunteers)
LT. KEITH KEREMSKI: 35-65
DET. MARK LINDSAY: 35-65

ACT I

Gary Greb, a Realtor and part-time comedian, has planned this caper for over a year and is finally satisfied (confidence built through comedy club performances) that he can pull it off.

11 SCENES
Settings: comedy club, real estate office, alley in Miami, title office, County Clerk's office, mortgage office, Miami home.

ACT II

5 SCENES
Settings: Apartment, comedy club, car lot, mortgage office, restaurant.

ACT III

6 SCENES
Settings: Bank, apartment, car dealership, Miami International Airport, police office.

ACT I
SCENE: 1

Setting: Comedy Club (*Stage left, or voices offstage*) Backstage, at a local Ft. Lauderdale comedy club. Various comedians are standing around backstage: but the focus is on Gary Greb, who, dressed as an Arab Sheik, has makeup on his face and hands to darken them considerably and wears a white turban wrapped tightly around his head, a silk shirt, open at the neck to reveal numerous gold chains and has several gold bracelets on his right wrist and what looks like a Rolex on his left, along with several rings with glistening gemstones.

(*Center Stage*) **M.C.:** Ladies & Gentlemen we have a visit tonight from an Arab Sheik. I know nothing about him so here he is: Sheik Mohammad El Faq."

Gary Greb: Yee-uzz pee-pills, I yeem Mohammad El-Faaa-ockcah. **SHEIK** Mohammad El-Faq-gah and I yeem a zeel-you-nair, so, you want to maybe to 'ear a foo-nee joke? You weel laugh or I weel buy zees play-sah and keeck you all out. (*subdued laughter*)

(*He does five more minutes of jokes and exits amidst resounding laughter. When he is approached by a fellow comedian who fails to recognize him his confidence skyrockets with an ear-to-ear smile, towards the audience.*)

SCENE 2:

Setting: (*Center Stage*) A title office in Ft. Lauderdale.

Gary Greb: Hey Liz, who's the closer?
Elizabeth Elkins: (*proffers a be-jeweled hand and exhales a noxious stream of cigarette smoke.*) Gary, how ah you, sweetie? It's Jeff Baker, do you know him darling? He's a very outgoing and colorful closer?
Greb: I know him; he's an outgoing and colorful sissy. (*shake hands*)
(*Beat*)
Elkins: Oh Gary, you naughty thing you.
(*The buyers & sellers come into the room and they all make small-talk until the closer arrives. Baker, sweeps into the room like a 300-lb. Richard Simmons. He hands Greb and Elkins each three folders and they hand their clients each one.*)
(*Pause*)
Jeff Baker: Well, shall we begin then everyone? This firs' page is the HUD-1, ah, the settlement statement and on line one-oh-one you will see the contract sales price of one hundred and two thousand dollars.
Greb: Say Baker, 'id jew get the que-cee?
(*Beat*)
Baker: The Q-wah Cee, excuse me Mistah Greb?
Greb: The quit-claim deed—I sent you one, remember?
Baker: Of caw-sah and it is in here. How else could we close? I do know my job. Now then if you will all please turn to ...
Greb: (*Winks at Elizabeth Elkins and yawns.*) Yeah, turn to ...
(*Light fades from scene slowly and comes up on other side of stage.*)

SCENE 3

Setting: Seedy part of Miami.

Gary Greb: (*glances nervously around, as a swarthy man nods at him.*) Hey man, you ah-er ...
Swarthy man: You got the mown-nee, mahn?
Gary Greb: Yeah, here's the picture and name and address too. (*Greb hands the man a hundred dollar bill and a card with a name and address on it, along with a wallet-sized photo and he disappears inside a dilapidated building, just around the corner from the Miami courthouse.*)
(*Pause*)
Swarthy man: Here it ees mahn. (*He hands Greb a Florida driver's license with the picture of Greb, dressed as an Arab Sheik on the front with the name Sheik Mohammad El-Faq.*)

SCENE 4

Setting: Greb's real estate office

Gary Greb: (*Sitting at desk practicing forging Mohammad Faisal's signature. Door opens and another realtor walks in.*) Ah-er-um, hey Terry. Wha ... ah ... 'uhts up?
Teresa Mann: Gary, I didn't know you were back here?
(*Beat*)
Gary Greb: Yeah, well, I'm just catchin' up on some work, y'know Tee, heh.
Teresa Mann: Did you know the door was locked?

(*Beat*)
Gary Greb: Ah, no, I didn't. Well, sorry but I gotta go.
(*Beat*)
Teresa Mann: Gary, do you have any que-cees? There's none in here, in the filing cabinet?
(*Beat*)
Gary Greb: (*Grabs the quit claim deed he had just practiced forging Muhammad Faisal's signature on and shoves it and several others into the waste basket.*) Nope, sorry Terry.
(*Beat*)
Teresa Mann: (*frowns, as the front door closes and she is still looking in filing cabinet*) I could of swore I put a stack of que-cees in here yesterday.

SCENE 5

Setting: Inside palatial Miami residence

Swarthy Arab: (*picks up ringing phone*) Mohammad Faisal residence.
Gary Greb: Eh, 'ello, eez dee Sheek en-ah plee-eze-zah?
(*Beat.*)
Swarthy Arab: Eh? No, who ees these, please?
Gary Greb: Moe-ham-ed Eel-Fack, I have beeznuz weeth Meester Fy-zell.
Swarthy Arab: Aw, I see, I am sorry but the Sheik is in Saudia Arabia until the first of next month.
Gary Greb: Hokay, I shall call heem then, Ah saalam ah lincolm.
Swarthy Arab: Hah! Ah saalam ah lincolm, brother.

SCENE 6

Setting: Title Company

Gary Greb: (*Dressed as Arab Sheik Mohammad El Faq; walks into office.*) 'ello.
Title Clerk: Ah, hello sir what can I do for you?
Gary Greb: Yes-ah, I am Mohammad El Faq and I need thees queet-claim deed notarized, please.
(*Beat*)
Title Clerk: (*Looking at the deed*) Well, Mr. El Faq ... uh, I will need to see some eye-dee please?
Gary Greb: Oh certainly, (*pulls out wallet, making sure the title clerk sees a wad of (dollar) bills stuck in between two hundred-dollar bills.*) Here you are then. (*Greb withdraws the forged driver's license from the same compartment and the quit-claim deed was quickly notarized*) Here, thees is for your trouble Mees.
(*Beat*)
Title Clerk: Oh my Gawd, a hundred dollars oh, I couldn't accept this.
Gary Greb: Don't worry, take it, take it please, for your time, your trouble.
(*Pause*)
Title Clerk: Oh well, (*glances around nervously*) thank you so much. (*Takes bill*)

SCENE 7

Setting: Dade County Clerk's office.

Gary Greb: *(Handing the clerk the bogus quit claim* deed.) Eh, could you reecor-ah a queet-claim deed for me, plee-sah?
(Beat)
Clerk: Certainly, sir, by the way there is a small recording fee, sir. (*Looks at the quit-claim deed, which she sees is already notarized and transfers property owned by Mohammad Faisal to Mohammad El-Faq.)*
Gary Greb: *(Handing her a hundred-dollar bill)* Here you are.
Clerk: Yes-sir, I'll just get your change.
Gary Greb: Keep it, plee-sah and could I get a copy plee-suh?
(Beat)
Clerk: Sir, for a tip like this you can get *anything* you want.
(Pause)
Gary Greb: *(Raises eyebrows so audience sees.)* Oh, reee-leee eets no-theeng ree-lee.
Clerk: (*Handing Greb a receipt, a photocopy of the recorded original quit-claim deed and 92 dollars in cash)* Here you are then, sir.
Gary Greb: *(pushing the 92 dollars back in her hand)* No please, take eet, really.
(Pause)
Clerk: Oh my and I thought you were just joking.
(Beat)
Gary Greb: No, I wasn't take eet please.
Clerk: Oh, well, then, thank you soooo much.
Gary Greb: *(Again, raises eyebrows towards audience.)* No problem Meees, no problem. *(He walks outside and raises his fists, holding in a scream. He puts the copy on top of a plat map on a clipboard he's carrying, showing a 56-acre parcel in Ft. Lauderdale that has an appraised value of fifteen million dollars and had been purchased in 1990 by Mohammad Faisal, for 6 million, and was now owned, on paper, by none other than Mohammad El Faq, a.k.a., Gary Greb.)*

SCENE 8

Setting: Gary Greb's real estate office.

Teresa Mann: (*Sitting on top of Greb's desk looking at all the quit-claim deeds that had been the recipient of Grebs' practiced forgeries. She sees several plat-maps of Mohammad Faisal's property in his desk drawer and is stymied.*) What the hell is Gary up to? (*a look of perplexity.*)

SCENE 9

Setting: Phone conversations from Greb's apartment to Mortgage Company and car lot.

Receptionist: (*Picks up ringing phone*) Max Mortgage, this is Ann, how can I help you please?
Gary Greb: Lemme speak with James Garen.
(*Beat.*)
Secretary: This is Diane, how can I help you please?
Gary Greb: James Garen and this is important aw-rye?
(*Beat*)
Diane: Sir, I am sure it is, whom shall I say is calling?
Gary Greb: Greb, Gary Greb. (*Elevator music reverberates*)
James Jonathon Garen III: (*desk phone rings*) Yes Di', what tiz it … I'm quite busy?
Diane: A Mister Greb on line three sir.
Garen: Tell him I'm in a meet-teeng Di'.
(*Pause*)
Diane: I'm sorry sir but Mister Garen is in a meeting. Would you like to leave a message?

Greb: Yeah, tell that fruit that if he don't…(S*hakes head and stares at the now-dead phone-line.*) Shit. Shee-it. Damn. *(Grabs the phone and stabs out seven numbers.)*
David Reed: (*car salesman*) Lox Lexus, diz is David Reed, how can I help youse?
Greb: Hey man, lemme speak tah Jackie Brown.
(*Beat*)
David Reed: Lemme see if I kin get 'im, hey iz diz Gary Greb?
(*Beat*)
Greb: Yeah, sup man?
David Reed: Hey, how's t'ings, youse still sellin' houses G-Man?
(*Pause*)
Greb: Yeah, man. Is Jackie there, Dave? (*Frowns.*)
(*Beat*)
Reed: Lemme see if dat shystah is aroun', jes' a sec' G-Man. He puts Greb on hold and a local easy listening channel comes on.
(*Pause*)
Brown: Hey, G-Man, what's up?
Greb: Jackie, hey man, you got any of yah old lawyer friends still? Maybe somebody hooked into a bank or loan company?
(*Beat*)
Brown: Well, maybe, G-Man? What kinna bank or loan company? You need some green, huh?
(*Beat.*)
Greb: (*exhales audibly.*) Not me, look I gotta client who's lookin' to get a loan on some property.
(*Beat*)
Brown: Shee-it G-Man, you know more brokers than I do.
(*Beat*)
Greb: But you know the movers and shakers in this town, Jack-oh.
(*Beat.*)
Brown: Naw, ever since I was disbarred it's like they never knew me. You think I like sellin' cars?

Greb: (*smiles despite his anxiety.*) Cars … hah …cars you say?
(*Beat.*)
Brown (*laughs*) I mean pre-owned vehicles, of course, and you know my offer still stands, a hundred clams you send me a buyer.
Greb: Yeah, look man I need ar-rah-um, like a big loan.
(*Beat*)
Brown: *You* do, huh?
Greb: I mean my client does Jay-Bee.
(*Pause*)
Brown: (*lights a cigarette and blows a stream of noxious smoke through his nostrils.*) What you up to, Gare?
(*Beat*)
Greb: Nothin' man. Look, I got this client, an Arab, dude owns a billion dollars worth of land and he wants some quick cash on a large piece.
Brown: How much cash, G-Man?
(*Pause*)
Greb: Ummm, well, about ah, rah-er—ten mil'.
(*Pause*)
Brown: (*Turns to audience and looks surprised, then egocentric and sarcastic.*) Ssssh, a big commish' for somebody, huh G-Man?
(*Beat.*)
Greb: Yeah, well, look, gimme a name, and I'll definitely make it worth your while Jackie.
Brown: Really Gee-Gee. (*in a falsetto voice.*)
Greb: C'mon Jackie, stop jerkin' me!
(*Beat*)
Brown: Man, I dunno nobody's got access to that kind of money. Well, except, of course ...
(*Beat*)
Greb: Except who, c'mon I'll make it worth your while Jamie.
(*Beat*)
Brown: Yeah right! (*sarcastic voice*)
Greb: Jackie, I will, man, Shee-it.

Brown: Well, Big Gee, Garen is the only one that I …
Greb: C'mon Jackie, everybody knows that sissy is plugged in. You think I'm gonna go to him? Hah, or is it her?
Brown: Who else you got? Where'd you ever get an Arab this rich?
(*Beat.*)
Greb: Just tryin' Jack, you know?
(*Beat*)
Brown: (*Frowns: all his senses tell him Greb is holding out. Then he sees a customer.*) Gotta go Gare.
Greb: Jackie, how about gettin' ahold of Garen for me? I'll make it worth your while?
(*Beat*)
Brown: (*inhales a lungful of smoke.*) C'mon G-Man, what're you up to? Don't bullshit me.
(*Beat*)
Greb: (*frowns*) Nothin' Jackie, I just got this deal and …
Brown: Look, I got a customer. Call me in an hour and we'll talk about that sissy Garen.
Greb: (*Rings off and bangs his fist on a table. He paces the room, then impulsively picks up the telephone and punches in seven numbers.*) Damn it I gotta ...
Femine Voice: Max Mortgage, can I help you, please?
(*Pause*)
Greb: Mister Garen, please.
Voice: Hold, please.
Different Voice: Mister Garen's office.
Greb: (*effeminate voice*) Oh, coo I speak with Jam-me, ple-zooh.
Voice: Certainly Mister Henley, would you hold, please.
Greb: Oh, sue Ah will.
Garen: (*Comes on the line almost immediately.*) Hon' what is it?
(*Beat.*)
Greb: Lis'en Garen, this is Gary Greb.
Garen: Wha' … what …? You have some nerve, I oughta ...

Greb: Before you hang up hear me out, man.
(*Beat*)
Garen: You've got egg-zact-lee thirty seconds.
Greb: I got a client who owns fifty-six acres out in West Broward and the dude needs some cash, quick.
(*Pause*)
Garen: How much cash are we talkin' about?
Greb: Ten mil'.
(*Pause*)
Garen: (*inhales quickly, realizing the brokerage fee alone will be in the six figures.*) Who is this client?
Greb: Mohammad El Faq. Look man, he's Faisal's brother-in-law.
(*Beat.*)
Garen: (*stands up on unsteady legs.*) Has it been appraised?
Greb: Fifteen-mil' and I got the package right here, I could have it in your office in an hour.
Garen: How about this Fugg guy, is he a sheik too?
(*Beat*)
Greb (*Smiles. Garen figures he's the only game in town because he is known by so many realtors to be accessible, greedy and connected to almost unlimited funds.*) I don't think he's a sheik, but look, he's in town now and he needs this large amount of money.
Garen: If the appraisal's right I can probably get him twelve.
(*Beat*)
Greb: (*shaking his head, then holds hand over receiver and whispers to himself, turns to audience:*) Talk about greed. Yeah, he might agree to it, man. Should I, ah, how you wanna do this?
(*Beat*)
Garen: Bring the package by—I'll be here.
(*Garen rings off and Greb exhales a stream of air. He goes to his closet to get a suit. His thousand dollar sharkskin suit hangs in the corner, the plastic wrapping from a recent dry-cleaning still*

covering it. Greb smiles and grabs it, holding it out in front of him. Looks and smiles at audience.) See this, a thousand bucks fer this baby but this is for later, this is for the coup de grace, yeah. *(puts it back in the closet and reaches for an old blue suit. He sits the blue suit on his bed and holds his hand out; it's shaking uncontrollably. He opens and closes his fist and it finally stops shaking. He rubs his hands together and realizes they are soaking wet with sweat and his undershirt is stuck to his skin. He runs to the bathroom, stripping his clothes off as he goes. He needs a cold shower before confronting Garen. As he turns the water on, one thought races through his mind and he verbalizes it.)* This is it, the most important performance of my life. Errr, I better not miss my marks this time, 'cause there ain't gonna be no second chance. *(Light fades out.)*

SCENE 10

Setting: Am-Core Building, where Max Mortgage has a suite, receptionist desk *(Center Stage)*

Greb: *(Walks to the secretary's escritoire. She smiles up at him)* I'm here to see James Garen, ah-er, I have a …
Secretary: Are you Mister Greb?
Greb: Ah, yuh, yes, yes I am.
Secretary: Mister Garen will be with you shortly, Mister Greb.
Greb: Oh, yeah, thanks.
Secretary: You can just have a seat, sir.
Greb: Yeah, sure. *(Puts briefcase next to a large leather sofa and sits down. The table in front of him is filled with several rows of*

magazines. Greb sees the Wall Street Journal and pushes it aside to reveal Forbes magazine and sees the others are all similar in nature; all dealing with money matters, stocks, interest rates, or some form of investment or tax advantage. He glances at the secretary and frowns. After a prolonged wait, clock shows 30 minutes goes by, Greb walks to the receptionist desk to complain, just as a door opens and another secretary nods at Greb.) Ummm, ah I'm ...

Diane (*Garen's secretary.*) Mister Greb. Mister Garen will see you now, just follow me. (*Greb follows her to a desk where she sits down at a computer and points towards a half-open door.*) Oh, you can go right in, Mister Greb. They're expecting you.

Greb: *(Notices a television screen on the secretary's desk and, as he approaches Garen's door suddenly realizes it was monitoring the outer office, where he had sat waiting for almost a half-hour.)* Hey, Mr. Garen.

(*Beat*)

Garen: Come right in, Mr. Greb. *(Recognizes Garen's silky voice and strolls in, his outward demeanor belying the butterflies in his stomach. Takes Garen's limp, outstretched hand. Sees another bulky man sitting in a chair opposite Garen's desk.)* This is Mr. Steven Lattner, Mister Greb. *(they shake hands.)* We checked the parcel ourselves, Steve owns several title companies. (*Greb is holding the plat-map and appraisal, along with a copy of the quit claim deed in his hand and Garen snatches it from him.*) We know this Mohammad El-Fugg guy owns the property, now. Steve was just saying that he did business with him before.

Greb: *(smiles despite himself and turns towards Lattner.)* Oh, really, huh?

Lattner: Yes I have, you see, I've known the sheik, for, for several years now.

(*Beat*)

Greb: Mohammad El Fak is the sheik's brother-in-law.

Garen: I'm well aware of that and also that he wants some quick cash, huh?

Greb: Yeah, said somethin' 'bout a gift for a *girlfriend*. (*Puts an obvious emphasis on girl and smiles at the audience.*) (*Pause.*)

Lattner: (*Clears his throat.*) Well, how much did **YOU** expect out of this?

(*Beat.*)

Greb: (*smiles. He had to play it right. He knew they figured they didn't need him and would cut him out at the first chance; exactly as he had planned it, and what he did next would make or break his deal: it was a critical performance.*) I was thinking one point.

(*Beat.*)

Garen: (*Looks at Lattner, jumps up.*) What? Are you crazy? We don't have to give you anything.

Lattner: Siddown Jay. And shaddup. (*Garen falls back into his chair like he had been shot and Greb sees who has control of the purse-strings.*) Mister Greb. Let's say I give you the point, when can you deliver Mister ElFugg?

Garen (*sneers st Greb*) Yeah, how do you know him? Where's a copy of a listing agreement or any contract between you two? Why would he go to you? Why should **WE** believe **YOU?**

(*Beat*)

Greb: (*Looks towards Lattner, now was the time, it was now or never. Pulls a business card from his pocket that had cost him a hundred dollars. They only printed them five hundred at a minimum and he had gotten the best. He hands it to Lattner.*) There's his business card. I met him. I know the man, he mentioned to me ... I mean he, that is, he, he asked me, he hired, he doesn't want to, ah-rah, um-ah, you know wire back home, see this girl is ... ah-rah, he doesn't really want to bother his brother-in-law, he told me, I'm telling you I have his confidence.

Lattner: (*Looks at Garen sharply*) We don't *need* this guy. (*Greb glares at both men then charges Lattner. He swats at his hand but misses, by a centimeter. The card slips out of Lattner's hand and*

Greb goes after it but Garen steps on it. He bends down just as Greb grabs his shoe. Garen kicks at Greb and his shoe collides with the side of Greb's head. Greb falls to the floor where he lays still until Lattner grunts and smiles.) I think you'd better leave Mister Greb.
(*Pause*)
Greb: (*Gets to a standing position and smiles thinly.*) You faggots, gimme the card; it is *my* card!
Garen: John, show Mister Greb out.
(*Beat*)
Greb: (*turns toward a rent-a-cop, security guard, now standing in the door-way.*) I'm not leavin' without the card, he's got my card? (*Glares at the cop, who turns toward Lattner and Garen.*)
(*Beat*)
Lattner: Show him the door, John.
(*Beat*)
Greb: (*Glares at Lattner, then Garen, but holds his hands up as the cop comes toward him*) Al-rye, al-rye, I'm goin', I'm goin'. (*At the door, he turns towards Lattner.*) He ain't gonna do nothin' with you sissy's anyway, I'll go see my man Jackie Brown. (*Greb smiles, hoping he hasn't overdone it.*)
Lattner: (*As door closes Lattner hands the card to Garen.*) It gives a business number and a beeper number.
Garen: (*rubs the card.*) Jackie Brown couldn't borrow a dime.
(*Beat*)
Lattner: The disbarred lawyer?
Garen: He got caught with his finger in Baud's trust fund. He almost did jail-time.
Lattner: What's he doin' now?
(*Beat*)
Garen: Heh-heh, last I heard he was sellin' cars.
Lattner: Let's call this Ay-rab, Jay. What do you say?
Garen: (*smiles and picks up his cellphone. It was a rather bulky 3 Watt cellphone with an antennae on the top. After trying twice,*

he puts it down. Finally gets it, leaves a short message. Looks at Lattner, then at the cellphone, and frowns)* These damn things, you'd think they could make them easier to use. Ah, they'll never catch on, too damn much anyway, two grand, hell the car-phone cost us half that.
(Beat)
Lattner: *(Frowns at the cellphone and shakes his head)* You're right there Jamie, cell-phones'll never catch on with anybody smart, they're junk and will only get worse; they need to shit-can them all now.
Greb: *(Walks out the front door when his beeper goes off. He checks the number, 978-1545, and smiles, Max Mortgage. He had only been wrong about one thing. It wasn't his best performance, that was yet to come. Turns to audience and smiles.)* I got 'em now, I got 'em!

SCENE 11

Setting: Real Estate office.

Teresa Mann: *(Stares at Gary Greb's empty desk, frowning. He hadn't been back in the office since she had discovered the forged quit claim deeds and he either wasn't home or wasn't answering his phone. She stands up, grabs her purse, and decides to stop at Greb's apartment building: being his ex-girlfriend she knew exactly where it was.)* I'm going to find out just what he's up to, one way or the other.

ACT II

SCENE 1

Setting: Greb's apartment.

Greb: (*Running to his front door he opens it to see two phones, sitting next to each other. One, a red phone, is, exclusively, Mohammad ElFaq's business line. He has an answering machine hooked to it and the light is blinking. Walking to it, Greb pushes the message button and his high falsetto voice, his impersonation of a Muslim secretary, resonates throughout his living room. When the beeper goes off and Garen's whiny voice comes on, Greb smiles, for it is what he has been waiting for, for almost two days. Garen mumbles that he is an acquaintance of Mohammad Faisal's and that he is available for consultation on any financial matter that the sheik may wish to discuss, specifically a loan on a piece of property that he has heard, through a friend, that the sheik might be in the market to mortgage. Greb waits for two hours until, finally, the phone rings again and he answers on the third ring.*) Yeah, 'low.
Garen: Oh, hel' ... hello. Is, ah-um, Mister El-lah-fack in please? (*Pause.*)
Greb: (*Recognizes Garen's shaky voice and grits his jaws. He was on and it wasn't a time to miss any of his marks.*) I eem Moe-ham-ed El-Faq what can I do for you sir?
Garen: Yes Mister El-lah-Fack, this is James Garen, I'm with Max Mortgage. (*A strained pause ensues but Greb stays silent.*) Well, ah-rah-ah, that is, I was wondering if you ah-er, you know might perhaps be interested in a mortgage on maybe one of your properties?

(*Beat.*)
Greb: Who 'ave you-ah talked to? I yeem een the market for a mortgage, I'm shopping right now.
Garen: Well, we heard that and we could offer you a very attractive rate.
Greb: I yeem shopping for a good rate my frien' and also, I need a large beet-ah of moo-nee. I have a parcel out in West Broward, my brother-een-law and I exchanged for a parcel back een Ree-ay-dah.
Garen: Of course, ah-er, how much would you need?
(*Beat.*)
Greb: Well, of course zee rate eez critical, also.
Garen: Oh, we'll beat any rate in town. What have you been offered?
Greb: Well, Abdul A-Zee-eez says he can get me seven and one-half.
(*Pause.*)
Garen: *(Scribbles seven and one-half on a piece of paper and Lattner smiles.)* I will give you seven.
Greb: (*Smiles.*) Well, then, where ees your off-eece?
Garen: (*Gives the address and Greb acts as if he's writing it down and then tells Garen he knows where the building is.*) And how much would you be needing, sir?
Greb: Ten meel-yun, my frien'.
(*Beat.*)
Garen: *(gasps and feigns surprise.)* Well, sir, we can possibly do business, could you give me the parcel number? We'll do a property analysis and should be able to have the money, if everything checks out, within twenty-four hours.
Greb: *(gives the information and this time Garen pretends to write it down.)* Well, that ees good then, you weel call me, then?
(*Beat.*)
Garen: Yessir, do you have another number?
Greb: *(smiles and gives the beeper number he knows Garen*

already has, on the business card.) You weel call me when you have the moonee, then?
Garen: Oh yes sir, we certainly will. *(Hangs up and frowns at Lattner.)* Who's this Abdul Aziz? I wonder if ElFugg'll take more money?

SCENE 2

Setting: Comedy Club.

Teresa Mann: *(Has seen Greb leaving his apartment and follows him to a local Ft. Lauderdale comedy club. She knows he used to do comedy bits around town for a few hundred dollars in the mid-80's and into the nineties. She walks into the club and the doorman asks her for I.D. She is 40 years old and smiles.)* Well, thank you for the compliment. *(The doorman smiles and lets her into the club just as she spots Greb talking to a bartender.)*
Bartender: Hey man, you goin' on tonight?
Greb: Maybe, who's the m-ah-cee?
Bartender: Ralph Williams, man, you want a drink?
(Beat.)
Greb: Gimme a rum 'n' coke, man.
Bartender: Sure thing. *(Places drink in front of Greb)*
Greb: *(nods at a man with shoulder length hair who steps up to the bar)* Hey Ralph.
Ralph: *(the M.C.)* Say man, you wanna do a set tonight?
(Beat.)
Greb: Yeah Ralph, put me on first.
Ralph: You got it baby.
Bulky Man *(club manager nods at Greb and then turns to Williams.)* Time to get it started Ralph.
Ralph: Soon's I get my med-sin.. *(To bartender)* The usual Max.

Greb: *(looks at bartender)* Tough audience.
(Beat)
Bartender: *(Laughs)* You're tellin' me, G-man?
Ralph: *(Moves to microphone, center stage.)* Our first performer is a real kidder. He's aggressive, so be ready. And here he is, Gary Jay Kidding.
Greb: *(strolls to the stage, takes the microphone off the stand and goes right into his old routine.)* Hey, how yah doin', my name is Gary J. Kidding, the jay stands for Justin but we shortened it to Just when I was just a kid and I been just kiddin' ever since, so don't take nothin' I say serious. Hey, I was born in New York but I grew up all over the country, actually all over the world 'cause my dad was in the service. Yeah Texas, Guam, England, Japan, yeah most of my time though I spent growin' up in a small African nation, yeah, maybe you heard of it, Washington, D.C. heh-heh. *(Audience laughs and Greb plows on. He does five more minutes of his regular routine then does his Arab impersonation. The audience loves it and Greb does almost five minutes as Mohammad ElFaq, the zillionaire who was going to buy the world and and then foreclose on it and he exits amidst laughter and applause. He goes to the bar to get a refill on his long finished rum and coke, and is surprised to see Teresa Mann, sitting at the bar, wearing a red miniskirt that was hiked up to where you could see her dark red under-panties and Greb sits down next to her)* Hey Tee, wah'sup?
Teresa Mann: You were really good Gary, funny.
(Beat.)
Greb: Yeah, how'd you like the Ay-rab impersonation?
Teresa Mann: If I'd of closed my eyes, I wouldn't have known it was you.
(Beat.)
Greb: Here, lemme buy you a drink T?
Teresa Mann: *(Smiles at Greb and rubs his thigh)* Oh thank you sweetie.

SCENE 3

Setting(s): Greb's apartment; car dealership, Max Mortgage Company: all telephone conversations.

Greb: *(Looks at clock and sees its 9:11 A.M. Has a hangover and when he staggers out of bed the covers fall to the floor, exposing a sinewy, shapely, sun-tanned thigh belonging to none other than Teresa Mann. Greb is relieving himself when the phone rings.)* Eeh El-lah Fack-ah Enterprises.
Voice: Oh, I have the wrong number, I'us lookin' for Gary Greb. *(Beat.)*
Greb: *(Greb rubs his hand over his whiskered face and notices he is on his phone, not the recently installed 'ElFaq phone and laughs.)* Who's this? Jackie?
Voice: Hey G-man, what's with the El-Fag Enterprises shit? *(Beat)*
Greb: Just jerkin' yah off Jackie, sup, man?
Jackie Brown: Just callin' to see if you want me to call that sissy Garen for you?
(Pause.)
Greb: (*Shakes his head in an attempt to clear the cobwebs in his brain and wonders how much he had let Jackie Brown in on.)* Aw, yeah, hey let's get together for lunch man, whaduhyuh say? *(Beat)*
Jackie Brown: Sure G-man, jus' come by the dealership around lunchtime I'll, ah-um try to break free of my heavy schedule.
Greb: Yeah, yeah, Jackie, I'll see yah later then, huh?
Jackie Brown: Aw-rye Gare, see yah at noon. *(Light fades from car lot, back to Greb's apartment.)*
Greb: *(Puts phone down and glances at Teresa Mann. She*

appears to be sleeping; her eyes are closed but her ears are wide open. The phone rings but this time it's the red phone, the ElFaq phone. Greb picks it up on the second ring.) Eeh, 'ello, dees ees ElFack-ah Enter-au -prises.

Garen: (*Light on Garen's office.*) Hello, is Mister ElFack in? This is James Garen.

(*Pause*)

Greb: (*Glances at Teresa Mann.*)Yeest a mee-nit, sir. (*Changes voice*) Eeh, thees-ah ees Moe-ham-ed Eel-Fack-ah.

Garen: Ah Mister ElFack, this is Jamie Garen. Max Mortgage.

Greb: Oh yes-ah , Meester Gar-reen , how are-ah you thees morneeng?

Garen: Very well thank you and we have your money available now, sir.

(*Beat.*)

Greb: Reel-lee, at what rate was that, again, Meester Gay-reen?

Garen: Ah-er, seven percent.

Greb: Seven percent then you-ah say. Well, are the papers ready?

(*Beat.*)

Garen: Ah-rah, we, we can have them ready in an hour.

Greb (*Glances at his watch, a quarter after nine.*) Well-ah, then-ah, I weel come up and sign them-ah.

Garen: Ah, what time should I expect you then, sir?

(*Beat.*)

Greb: Oh, cup-pull ah hours-ah, I weel be there by eleven.

Garen: Fine, we'll expect you around eleven, then, sir. We'll have the papers all ready and the funds will be available at ten million then?

Greb: Yee-es-sah, teen ees good.

Garen: Well, because *we could have **TWELVE*** available, at the same rate, of course.

(*Beat.*)

Greb: Twelve, you say, maybe I weel take twelve at seven. I will theenk eet over Meester Gareen if you have twelve available for

me you say?
(*Beat.*)
Garen: Oh well, okay then, we'll definitely have it available.
Greb: Hokay, then, Ah saalam ah lincoln, brother.
Garen: Ah, yes sir Ah salum, then ah goodbye then, sir. (*Puts phone down and smiles at Steve Lattner.*) You heard? I think he's gonna take the twelve.
Lattner: We're gettin' *TWO* points over par? This A-zeez guy must be makin' a killin' chargin' seven and a half points to these high-rollers. We're gettin' two points yield spread on this too, at twelve million that's what? Two hundred forty large, plus we got a load ah junk fees. Is he wise to yield spread, does he know about back-end money? Is he gonna go for that? These Ay-rabs're usually slicker'n that.
Garen: C'mon Steve, he knows there's always an origination fee and the junk fees are just part of that. He's too rich to be checkin' the margin, okay? Anyway, seven percent is good for that amount of money and on such short notice? C'mon these Ay-rabs are rollin' in it, what's a couple ah points to a billionaire and, anyway, seven percent ain't gonna be beat unless they got insiders workin' for them, shhhh, a couple hundred grand to these guys is chickenfeed. This is money he's gonna throw away on his girlfriend anyway, right?
(*Beat.*)
Lattner: Yeah, you're right, come to think of it. (*Light fades, scene switches to Greb's apartment.*)
(*Pause.*)
Greb: (*moves his face closer to the bathroom mirror, and notices a scab just underneath his eye, where Garen had kicked him less than 24-hours ago.*) Gee-zuz I ain't gonna be ready in two hours.
Teresa Mann: Did you say something, honey?
(*Pause.*)
Greb: (*Glances over and sees Teresa Mann sitting up in bed.*) I gotta go out, you gotta get up baby, now. (*Greb moves quickly to*

his clothes closet and removes his thousand-dollar sharkskin suit. Fifteen minutes later, Greb walks Teresa Mann to a cab he has called and hands the driver a twenty, kisses her, then jumps in his car and speeds away. He pulls into Lox Lexus twenty minutes later without the slightest awareness of the cab parked just across the street, where, inside, Teresa Mann is inhaling a cigarette and watching the meter click up, every sixty seconds. She had heard the phone conversation but thought that Greb was trying to impersonate an Arab to get twelve thousand bucks and he had fallen considerably in her estimation.)

SCENE 4

Setting: Car lot of auto dealership.

Jackie Brown: (*Standing on the lot talking to fellow salesman David Reed when Brown sees Greb approaching them.*) Well-well, lookee here Davie.
David Reed: Hey G-Man, what's up?
Greb: (*nods at both men*) Say Dave, I need to talk to you Jackie.
David Reed: Hey G-Man, nice t'reads, wha' is it Ah-manee or Brooks Bruddahs?
Jackie Brown: G-Man, I thought we had a lunch date man. Sheeit, it's barely half past nine? Sup?
(*Beat.*)
Greb: (*shrugs his shoulders and tries to smile.*) Nothin' man, where's yah demo, man?
Jackie Brown: In the lot, where it always is G-Man … why?
(*Beat.*)
Greb: I need tah borrow it Jack-oh.
(*Beat*)

Jackie Brown: *Man, I'm wheelin' a ninety-six S-sah Cee four hundred, man with less than a grand on the odometer. Shee-it, Gary 'at's sixty grand on wheels, baby.*

Greb: Jackie, I need it. *(Pulls out a twenty dollar bill and hands it to Brown, full-well knowing it was the only language Brown understood.)* There's another twenty when I get back. I only need it for ah-nah 'bout ah hour, man.

Jackie Brown: *(Fingers the twenty, then hands it back to Greb.)* Hey, sorry G-Man but I just can't take the chance.

David Reed: *(Greb looks towards David Reed)* Shee-it … shee-it, G-Man, I'm drivin' a damn ate-tee t'ree L-lah-S four hun'red, man. Youse kin take it if youse want?

Greb: *(Scowls at Jackie Brown.)* Man, it's a broad, okay?

David Reed: A goil? Shit Jay-Bee, give 'im dah short.

(Beat.)

Greb: *(pulls out wallet and takes out everything in it. Stuffs two ones and a five in his pocket and hands Brown four twenties.)* Here man. There's another hundred in it when I get back.

Jackie Brown: *(Smiles and takes the four twenties.)* Well, yeah for four Andrew Jackson's well, but I dunno though G-Man?

David Reed: C'mon Jay-Bee, dah man gives yah four double-saws and a cee-note when he gets back, shee-it, diz goil mus' be a reg-you-lah Pamela Anderson.

(Beat.)

Jackie Brown: *(Smiles at Reed.)* Whose Pamela Anderson?

David Reed: Youse know man, Baywatch. Big titties.

Greb: *(Smiles at Jackie Brown.)* Man, dis broad's got tees like Dolly Parton and pins like Juliet Prowse, Jackoh.

Jackie Brown: *(Shakes his head and reaches into his pocket, hands Greb the keys.)* If you wreck it, G-Man, I'll say you were a customer.

(Beat.)

Greb: Sure, man, wanna photocopy my driver's license? I know you guys like to do that.

Jackie Brown: (*Scowls and walks Greb to his dark green Lexus sport coupe where they shake hands.*) It better be in the same condition when you bring it back, no scratches.
(*Beat*)
Greb: Thanks Jackie, I'll be back in a flash, I'll buy lunch.
(*Pause.*)
Jackie Brown: Just bring back my car, G-man. (*Greb nods and light fades away*).

SCENE 5

Setting: Garen's office.

Steve Lattner: Think he's gonna show, Jay-Gee? (*Both men are looking out the window, presumably at the parking lot*).
Jamie Garen: (*points out the window.*) Arggh-eh … I don't … oh, look Stevie, getting out of the Lexus, that's him?
(*Pause*)
Receptionist: Oh, hello, are you Mister ElFog.
Greb: Eh, yees I yam.
Diane: (*The receptionist is about to say something when the statuesque blonde Greb knows is Garen's private secretary appears suddenly, her stiletto heels clicking on the marble floor.*) Oh, Mister El-ah-Fack, Mister Garen and Mister Lattner are expecting you, sir. You may go right in, sir.
Greb: (*The door is half open and he walks in and Garen is all over him, sticking his pale limp hand forward.*) Mister ElFack, I am James Garen and this is my associate Mister Steven Lattner.
Lattner: (*Comes forward to grasp Greb's hand, stares him in the eye and squeezes his hand.*) Say, don't I know you?
(*Pause.*)
Greb: I don't the-eeenk so, my brother-een-law ees Mohammad

Faisal. Maybe ees heem you know? (*Greb smiles sickly and Lattner, who has done business with Faisal but had never met the man, smiles and nods his head slowly, his face taking on the appearance of one who has just made a remarkable discovery.*) (*Beat.*)
Lattner: Yes-yes, of course; you bear a striking resemblance.
Greb: The pay-peers please, gentlemen, I yam een a hurry.
Garen: Certainly sir, just have a seat right here. (*Garen gestures to his own plush chair behind his desk. Greb nods and slides behind the desk where Garen is standing. Garen leans down and points at the bottom line, where it calls for Mohammad ElFaq's signature.*)
Greb: Yes, I see eet, so, you have a *nice* commeession here, I see. (*Beat.*)
Garen: (*Grits his jaws and flashes a pained glance towards Lattner, whose nostrils flare open.*) Ah, yes … yah … yessir. I mean we stand to make ah-er-um …

Greb: (*Reaches for a pen on Garen's desk and signs with a flourish the fictitious signature of Mohammad ElFaq of ElFaq Enterprises, incorporated. He repeats the process on the sheaf of papers underneath, then hands the papers and pen to Garen.*) No problem my frien'. (*He withdraws a business card from his vest pocket and hands it to Garen.*) These ees my account number, the bank ees in Miami. When can you have the funds transferred?
Garen: Oh, we can do that right now, sir. We have a bank in this building. Just follow me?
(*Beat.*)
Greb: Certain-lee, Meester Gay-reen.
Lattner: (*The transfer is made and a bank account Greb had opened in Miami with a hundred-dollar bill was now eleven-million, 540-thousand dollars richer. Lattner and Garen watch as Greb gets into the Lexus.*) Let's go spend some of our hard-earned money, baby. (*Light fades away.*)

SCENE 6

Setting: Restaurant.

Teresa Mann: (S*miles at a friend, Diane, Garen's personal secretary, as they are eating lunch together in the Am-Core building.*) My but you look good Di', different, somehow?
Diane: *(Leans in towards Teresa)* I had them put in last month. You wouldn't believe the new interest all the men shower on me now Tee? (*Then Bramson glances at Mann's well-endowed bust-line and smiles.*)Well, I guess you do. They are *yours*, aren't they?
Teresa Mann (*Giggles.*) Yes but I wish I had your cheeks. (*A waiter sets down two glasses of ice-water and two menus and then leaves.*) Di', this Am-Core building is really impressive, I mean, it just reeks of money. How do you like working for James GAY-ren?
(*Beat*)
Diane: Oh, I know, everybody knows he's gay but Tee, the money that man has. God the people he deals with though are unreal.
(*Beat*)
Teresa Mann: Really, I mean … what do you mean?
(*Beat*)
Diane: I'll tell you what girl, my Gawd, you wouldn't believe what happened this morning. An Arab borrowed twelve million dollars, girlfriend.
(*Pause.*)
Teresa Mann: Wha' … wha' … what, an Arab, do you know his name? (*Mann looks totally startled*)
(*Beat.*)
Diane: Uh, Moe-ham-med, they're all Mohammad something, you know Tee? This one was special though, he was a sheik, can

you imagine? I remember, Sheik Mohammad ElFag, hah! Funny huh Tee? ElFag? I mean you know? It sounded like fag anyway, hah! Tee, what's wrong? You look like you've seen a ghost? (*Beat*)
Teresa Mann: Oh, my Gawd! (*Gasps and stands up, but before Diane Bramson says anything further or knew what was happening, Teresa Mann is running towards the door.*)

ACT III
SCENE 1

Setting: Miami Bank.

J. Paulding Smythe: (*Bank President*) We really appreciate your business Your Excellency.
Greb: (*Dressed as Mohammad El Faq.*) Think nothing of it sir and I will do all my future business here, you have been quite helpful.
J. Paulding Smythe: Oh, thank you, thank you Your Excellency.
Greb: "My pleasure Mr. Smythe, and I look forward to our future transactions. (*extends his hand and they shake and Smythe is all bows and scrapes as the door closes on Greb and he walks out of the bank building, on Biscayne Boulevard in Miami, with a smile on his face and a hundred and thirty thousand dollars in his pockets. Dressed as the sheik, he stops walking and, for barely an instant, it hits him; he has gotten away with it but he hasn't even any time to dwell on the fact that he has transferred eleven million, four-hundred thousand to his numbered account in the Cayman Islands and has closed that account by transferring it to a bank in Geneva, Switzerland; he had opened both accounts over a year ago, even though his lone sting operation had been*

little more than a pipe dream, then. He had taken the $130 grand more as proof of his conquest than an actual need for that much money. Planning to purchase a ticket to Geneva as soon as possible, it was only now starting to sink in that he had 11 million, 400 thousand awaiting his arrival in Geneva, Switzerland. He had left ten thousand dollars in the Miami bank with a promise to deposit more in the future and J. Paulding Smythe, the bank's president, and a man who had dealt in the past with Sheik Faisal himself, had been all bows and scrapes, for Sheik Faisal's brother-in-law, Mohammad El Faq, who, now patted his breast pocket where one-hundred crisp thousand-dollar bills resided, a circular paper band with the bank's name inscribed on it the only thing holding them together. He quickly walks to his double-parked Lexus. He sees a crippled Vietnam veteran and walks over.)

Greb: Hey man, how's it goin'? (*Puts ten one-thousand-dollar bills in his begging cup, a mayonnaise jar.*)

Vietnam Veteran: (*Moves his wheelchair forward and removes bills, then smiles at the audience.*) Uh, thousand-dollar bills, huh? Counterfeit, of course. Uh-ah, maybe I can trade them for something to eat anyway. (*Sticks them in his pocket.*)

SCENE 2

Setting: Greb's apartment.

Greb: (*Inside his apartment, takes a shower; then collapses onto the tile floor. Suddenly, Greb lets out an unbridled scream and then begins laughing hysterically, as it has finally sunk in; he had pulled it off, he had pulled it off just like he had planned to. The play had been played out and the player, Gary Greb, had won, he* had played the system again and had won again but this time, he had won big, so big he would never have to play the game, ever again. *Let's out a horrific scream and looks at the audience,)* Ah, did you see that? I did it, I did it, I did it, **I DID IT!**

SCENE 3

Setting: Auto dealership, car lot.

Teresa Mann: (*Glances at watch, she has been looking at cars for over an hour, in the Lox Lexus car dealership, waiting to see if Greb was going to show up. She has finally gotten rid of her salesman and gone into the ladies room. She hears that Greb has come onto the used car lot and hears him arguing with Jackie Brown.*)

Jackie Brown: (*Audience hears what Teresa Mann sees*) Ah matter wid you, I could lose my job, my demo G-Man, ... wha' ... (*Brown's eyes magnify like saucers and his lips part in a smile when he recognizes his God, as Greb hands him two bills.*) Two hundred, now you're talkin'.(*Looks at his demo.*) Hey, no scratches, cool.(*Then he looks at the two bills in his hand.*) Gee-zuz Gare, these're thousand dollar bills, two large? Gee'zuz G-Man, what the fugg? What'd you do?

Greb: (*Grabs Brown's elbow and steers him towards the wall, just the other side of the ladies room.*) Just tell the whole friggin' world, Jay-Bee, man, shit.

Jackie Brown: G-Man, what'd jew do, hold up a bank?

Greb: Somethin' like that man. I gotta go, Jack-oh.
(*Pause*)

Jackie Brown: Gary, c'mon, man. C'mon. What's up G-man,

c'mon man cut me in, I'll do anything?
(*Beat*)
Greb: Jackie, I'll call you man, I'm in a hurry, right now. (*Light fades away, darkens.*)
Teresa Mann: (*Light to bathroom, Teresa stands listening and hears Greb as he curses himself for giving Brown the two thousand and then sounds of his car pulling away. Teresa looks out and sees Jackie Brown standing in the middle of the car lot with his arms outstretched, pleading for Greb to let him in on the deal.*) Where is he going? (*Teresa runs out to follow Greb, who heads straight for the interstate and the Miami International Airport.*)

SCENE 4

Setting: Miami International Airport.

Jamacian Cabdriver: Hey, yah cah-not leave yah cah outside mon. (*Greb has left his battered Ford, bought just for this occasion, behind a taxi-cab, outside. The cab driver follows him into airport.*) Hey, yah cah-not leave yah cah outside mon. Hey yah can ...
Greb: (*Turns for an instant and smiles at the Jamaican cabbie. With $122,000 in cash in his pockets and $11-million, 400,000 awaiting him in Switzerland, Greb no longer cares.*) Keys are in it, its yours, do whatever you want with it. (*Greb quickly disappears one way and the cab-driver the other way.*)
Teresa Mann: (*Runs into the airport and spies Greb, hurries after him. She has left her car, with the keys in it, running, in the street. She bumps into a old man who spills his coffee but sees Greb and keeps running*) Oh, sorry, didn't mean to ...

SCENE 5

Setting: Ticket Counter.

Greb: *(Lays a crisp, thousand-dollar bill on the counter and is handed a one-way ticket to Geneva and change. Glances at his watch, almost 2:00 PM. His plane should be in the air in less than an hour. He pats his coat, just over the inside breast pocket where a Swiss bank-book resides along with an envelope containing forty-five, $500-dollar bills and ninety-eight $1,000-dollar bills. He is daydreaming of an idyllic life in Europe when he feels a body brush his and his name resounds into his ear. Looks up and sees Teresa Mann.)* Going to Switzerland, Gary?
(Beat.)
Greb: *(Does a double-take of the ticket-counter he had just come from and eyes Mann speculatively.)* "Wha' … where …?
(Beat)
Teresa Mann: Where's Mohammad El-lah-Fack, he around, somewhere?
(Pause)
Greb: What do you mean, Tee? What are you talkin' about?
Teresa Mann: Oh, come on Mister G-Man. I know you've got twelve-million bucks that you scammed from Max Mortgage.
(Pause)
Greb: *(His eyes became saucers and his mouth drops open. If she knew, who else knew? Were the cops closing in on him this very second? He looks around speculatively, then turns sullen and jerks Teresa's elbow, steering her into an airport restaurant.)* C'mon Tee, let's get somethin' to eat.
Teresa Mann: Oh, are you buying, Mister El-lah-Fack? *(The restaurant has a bar and it's empty. Greb takes an end-seat and Teresa Mann slides onto a stool.)* I can't believe you did it.
(Pause)

Greb: (*Lowers voice to a whisper*) I can't believe you know I did it. How did you … ah, how did ...
Teresa Mann: I found a dozen que-cees with Mohammad El Fack's name scribbled on 'em, in your waste-basket at work. That's when I first got suspicious.
(*Beat*)
Greb: You … you followed me. You set me up at the comedy club? (*Mann smiles and Greb scowls at the bartender.*) Rum'n'coke and a gin martini for the lady. (*The bartender, a bulky man with a look of desultory disinterest, nods and does an about-face. Teresa Mann smiles and snakes her hand onto Greb's thigh and leans forward: puts her mouth an inch from Greb's ear.*)
(*Beat*)
Teresa Man: Gary, we're good for each other. (*She snakes her tongue into his ear and he jumps backwards. With over eleven and a half million dollars awaiting his arrival in Geneva, he wasn't prepared for a long-term relationship. He nods at the bartender, who sits the two ordered highballs on the bar-counter, and pulls out a five-hundred dollar bill, laying it on the bar.*)
Greb: Kin yah change a Mah-Kin-lee?
(*Beat*)
Bartender: (*Smiles and takes the bill.*) Sure, man.
Teresa Mann: (*Frowns.*). Why Miami, I mean there's an airport in Fort Lauderdale?
Greb: Yeah but Miami's a jungle, so I left my car outside, running. What's the chance it would even be there when I came out? In Lauderdale, shee-it, they'd probably trace it through Dee-M-Vee. (*Greb reaches in his coat and lays down the envelope with, now, $117,500 in it, and removes a thousand-dollar bill and two five-hundreds, sliding them into his pocket.*) Look Tee, there's a quarter million bucks in there, in five-hundreds and thousands.
Mann: You're not buying me off so cheap, G-Man.
Greb: What? You'll never see this kinna green again. C'mon, what the hell do you want?

Teresa Mann: I want half, sweetie-pie.
Greb: Wha' … what … you gotta be kiddin'?
Teresa Mann: But baby. (*Mann coos and slides her hand between Greb's legs where he lets it remain.*)
Greb: (*Glances at the bartender, examining the five-hundred dollar bill under a small lamp, sitting next to a cash register and pulls out his Swiss Air ticket, handing it to Mann.*) Tell yah what, baby. Here, go and get yourself a seat close to mine.
(*Pause*)
Teresa Mann: (*Gasps and puts her hand on her breast. She massages it gently and shows Greb her capped teeth.*) Oh sweetie, you don't mean it?
Greb: Sure I do, can't beat 'em, join 'em, I always say. Look, Tee, does anybody else know about this?"
Teresa Mann: No, of course not, Gary, I thought you were trying to get twelve grand, at first, but then, well, I talked to Di.
Greb: Di?
Teresa Mann: Diane Bramson. She used to work for Triple Tee Realty when I was there, years ago. She's Garen's personal secretary.
(*Beat*)
Greb: Well, how did you … you mean that …?
Teresa Mann: She told me about Mohammad El-lah-Fack and his twelve mil-yun dollar loan.
(*Beat*)
Greb: Yeah, huh, well, go get yah a ticket.
Teresa Mann: Aren't you coming?
(*Beat*)
Greb: I gotta use the bathroom, bad. (*Teresa eyes the envelope full of bills, just as the bartender sits Grebs' change on the counter-top, four hundreds, four twenties and a ten and Greb follows her gaze.*) Take it with you.
Teresa Mann: (*Slips the envelope in her purse and Greb slips the four hundreds and four twenties in his pocket. He leaves the ten*

and nods at the bartender.) I'll go buy a ticket.
Greb: You do that baby. *(Turns to the bartender)* Keep the sawbuck, I'll be back after I take a leak
Bartender: Thanks man. *(Nods as Greb shoots off the stool and Teresa Mann joins him. She glances at the ticket.)*
(Beat)
Teresa Mann: We'd better get going, the plane leaves in forty-five minutes.
Greb: Yeah, we got plenty ah time baby, plenty ah time, Go get your ticket, c'mon, I gotta take a leak, I'll be right out. *(Greb is standing in a stall when the loudspeaker blasts an announcement of a plane due to leave in ten minutes, bound for Atlanta. He comes out and glances at the boarding gates, quickly makes a decision, and sprints towards them. He gets through easily and makes it to the gate he was looking for but there are only a half-dozen people left, waiting in the line to get on the plane. Greb walks to the line and approaches a middle-aged man with a ticket in his hand. He nudges his elbow.)* Hey man, you on flight five ninety-two, huh?
Man: Turns with a pained expression on his face. I am.
Greb: *(Pulls a roll of bills from his pocket.)* Look man, I ah-rah-er-um-ah, gotta get to Atlanta, an important business conference, you understand? Look, I'll buy your ticket; look here, five hundred bucks. *(Hands the man a five-hundred-dollar bill)*
Man: *(Has never seen a five-hundred-dollar bill before but he has seen a hundred. He smiles at Greb)* It's only a low-fare line, man. I ah-er, I only paid a little bit more than ...
Greb: *(Sees the man staring at the hundreds and twenties, and quickly hands them to him, with a smile.)* Here, take this and the five-hundred too. *(Offers his hand)* I'm Gary Greb, by the way.
Man: *(Shakes Greb's hand.)* Oh, yeah, I'm Bill, Bill Jeffers. *(Looks at the five-hundred-dollar bill, then the four hundreds and four twenties; ten times what he had paid for the ticket to Atlanta. Smiles at Greb and hands him the ticket. Greb exhales and*

laughs, takes the ticket and boards the plane.)
Greb: (*Smiles at stewardess as she leads him to his seat. A middle-aged man and woman are his neighbors and they stop talking when he sits down.*) How yah doin', Gary Greb?
Passengers: (*The man shakes Greb's hand and smiles. He introduces his wife and they make small talk. The man is telling Greb that he and his wife had just come from their second honeymoon in the Bahamas and were returning home to Atlanta.*) Yeah, I miss working. You believe that. I got a good rest though. Yup, I'm ready to go back to it, now.
Greb: (*Obviously uninterested.*) Yeah, wha' ah yah do?
Man: I drive a truck. Yup, I got my own rig, the Hope Express. My little girl's name is Hope.
Greb: Hey, that's nice man, I … (*Stares as if at a ghost but it is no ghost. Teresa Mann is being seated just across the aisle from him and she is smiling.*)
Teresa Mann: (*Raises her eyebrows at Greb and smiles.*) H'low Mohammad. (*Nods at the couple next to Greb.*) Mister Mohammad, he's rich; see, he's a scam artist who is also ...
Greb: (*Glares at Mann. She's in a window seat in an otherwise empty aisle-seat and Greb jumps up and sits next to her in an instant. Greb is whispering to her when a man walks up and stands in the aisleway staring at them both.*) Tee, look you gotta … what?
Man: I think you're in my seat, sir.
Greb: (*Looks up to the middle-aged man glaring down at them. Hands the man his ticket.*) Could you trade me, man. My wife and I couldn't seem to get adjoining seats, y'know?
Man: (*Grumbles until Greb hands him a hundred-dollar bill and smiles, then goes back to talking to Teresa.*) Well, okay then.
Teresa Mann: Mister El-lah-Fack there is only one hundred and eighteen thousand dollars in this envelope and you said a quarter of a million.
(*Beat*)

Greb: (*Frowns and whispers*) Shuddup, willyah Tee. One drink, and yer soused, Gee-zuz. (*Teresa Mann opens her mouth just as the loudspeaker clicks on and the captain announces that ValuJet flight 592, non-stop to Atlanta, would be departing soon and to fasten their seat-belts. As they taxi down the runway Gary Greb sits back in his chair and glares at Teresa Mann. But, then, he smiles and grabs her hand.*) Well, guess I'd better get used to you then, huh?

(*Beat*)

Teresa Mann: (*Scowls*) Gary, if you think ...

Greb: Naw, I mean it this time, Tee. Hey, lemme tell you how I did it, I been dying to tell somebody.

Teresa Mann: (*Grins and slips her hand onto Greb's thigh.*) I can't wait to hear it.

Greb: (*Is halfway through with his story when Teresa Mann wrinkles her nose.*) 'What is it Tee?

(*Beat*)

Teresa Mann: Gary, do you smell smoke?"

Greb: (*Inhales and looks up. A beefy man, dressed in a rumpled Brooks Brothers suit, stumbles down the aisle.*) What's up?

Man: There's a fire in the cabin.

(*Beat*)

Greb: I knew it, I should have waited 'till tomorrow. Sunday's a better day than Saturday. Eleven'n half mil' and we're gonna freakin' crash. I knew it, I knew it.

Teresa Mann: Gary, please wait a minute, don't talk like that.

Beefy Man: Shee-it, he's probably right. (*Beefy man in Brooks Brothers suit sways in the middle of the aisle.*) And I oughtah know, I flew one ah these suckers in ah war.

Greb: War, what war?

Beefy Man: Nam and these Dee-Cee-Nine's go down hard.

Teresa Mann: (*Pilot comes on loudspeaker, informing passengers that he is turning around and returning to M.I.A and Greb smiles when Teresa Mann pulls two Swiss-Air tickets from*

her purse.) Think we'll make our flight baby?
(*Beat*)
Greb: (*Glances at his watch. Twenty minutes after* 2:00 P.M. *Puts his hand between Mann's legs*.) We just might. (*Looks out the window and gasps.*) Gee-zuz, we're over the freakin' Everglades. (*Even as he says it, the big plane veers into a seventy-five degree downfall and quickly heads towards those Everglades. Greb inhales deeply and smiles at Teresa Mann.*)
Teresa Mann: (*Bats her eyes at Greb.*) "I luv you bay-bee, I do, I really do!
Greb: (*As the plane hits the muddy swamp, Greb smiles lopsidedly and says, the same thing over and over and over and over.*) I knew it, Tee, I knew it. My luck, my freakin' luck, I knew it, I knew it, dammit, **I KNEW IT!**

BLACKOUT or CURTAIN

SCENE 6

Setting: A police department, somewhere in Washington, D.C.

Lieutenant Keith Keremski: (*Smiles across desk at Detective Mark Lindsay. A stack of financial crimes files litters the top of his desk. It is late night, 9:00 PM and Keremski rubs his tired eyes; they have been on duty since early that morning and are ready to leave. It is just after New Year's, 2016, and Keremski and Lindsay are polishing off some left-over liquor. Both men have shots of bourbon, in small Styrofoam cups usually used for coffee, sitting on Keremski's cluttered desk. Lindsay closes a manila folder he's reading and throws it on a heap of the same. He sips the bourbon.*) Yeah, that Tommy True was somethin' else, huh

Mark? Dude had fifty-one known aliases. I think he was the king, man. Yup, ol' Tommy Tee would get my vote for the king of the sting, man. We got 'im on dozens of cons but he never did more than a couple days before that mouthpiece of his sprung 'im
Detective Mark Lindsay: Yeah, he had a good lawyer but remember none of the vic's could eye-dee Tommy Tee.
(*Pause*)
Keremski: Yeah, he sure had *some* disguises. I think his best disguise was himself in a three-piece suit in court. That's why they couldn't ever eye-dee 'im. Yeah, he was the king of 'em all, huh, Mark? Kin yah imagine 'im dyin' like that, a heart attack, in his sleep?
(*Beat*)
Lindsay: Yeah, crazy Keith, he was somethin' though, gotta admit, probably the King, huh?
(*Beat*)
Keremski: (*nods and sips his coffee. Glances at the folders on his desk. They were all old cases, all over a decade, many even two or three decades old. One caught his eye and it had* **'THE SHEIK,'** *in dark, bold letters on the lip. Keremski snatches it up and nods at his partner.*) Remember this one. (*Slides it to Lindsay, who opens it*)
(*Pause*)
Lindsay: Oh, shit! We never solved it. (*Takes a swallow of bourbon then grabs the bottle and pours another shot. He smiles and flips through the folder.*) *DAMN*! This guy was the real king. I mean sheik. We never even eye-dee'd the perp' in this case.
Keremski: Yeah, got away with like fifteen mil' if I remember correctly.
(*Beat*)
Lindsay: (*Nods as he peruses the file.*) Yeah, twelve, man, to think Keith, this guy's somewhere right now livin' like a king, shit a sheik, Sheik Mohammad El Faq. This guy disappeared like a ghost. Crime pays, huh Keith, shee-it, think we'll ever get him?

I mean the money disappeared.

(*Beat*)

Keremski: Yeah, it disappeared into that deep, dark hole known as the Bahamas, or the Caymans, or Switzerland. (*Reaches for the folder then throws it on a pile of similar cases that are all considered long dead and gone, the statute of limitations up, on many of them. He smiles at the stack, even as Lindsay frowns.*)

Lindsay: It's still in the system ain't it, Keith? I mean they didn't take it out of the computer yet, right?

(*Beat*)

Keremski: (*Chuckles slightly and frowns at Lindsay, whom he knew hated to see cases like this one closed. He takes the file from Lindsay.*) It's still in the system Mark but it's been almost two decades; believe me its dead.(*Keremski stands up and Lindsay stretches and yawns.*)

(*Beat*)

Lindsay: Yeah, it's dead. The king is dead, huh, shit, Tommy Tee had nothin' on this guy, whoever he was. Yeah, the king is dead, all right. (*Lindsay stands up and he and Keremski walk out of the squad room.*) As the door closes, Keremski smiles at his partner of nearly two decades.

(*Beat*)

Keremski: (*Throws the file on the desk.*) You only got one thing wrong, Mark. The king was actually a sheik. Yup, and the Sheik is dead, partner, the Sheik is dead.

END OF PLAY

(BLACKOUT or CURTAIN)

MY NAME IS NOBODY

AN ORIGINAL PLAY IN ONE ACT

CHARACTERS

JOE: Walmart greeter. Age 67
RICHARD: Beggar, paralyzed from waist down, in wheelchair. Age 50-65
MOLLY: Clean-up lady. Age 35-45.
JUAN: Farm-worker. Age 35-45
RUSSELL RED CLOUD: Native American janitor at Casino. Age 40-50.
BOBBY SYKES aka SHAKES: Jail inmate, Age 25-35.
PETE: Homeless man, age 55.
DONNA: Single mother. Age 25-30.
ROGER: Poor, bankrupt man. Age 35-45.
THREE HOMELESS VIETNAM VETS: Ages: 65-75
TWO COPS: Age 35-50

SCENE 1: Just inside front doors of a Wal-Mart.
SCENE 2: Same Walmart sidewalk in front of store. Same day.
SCENE 3: Inside an office. Same day.
SCENE 4: Picking fruit in a vineyard. Same day.
SCENE 5: Gambling casino. Same day.
SCENE 6: Jail-cell. Same day.
SCENE 7: Street corner. Same day.
SCENE 8: Food Store. Same day.
SCENE 9: Inside a church. Same day.
SCENE 10: A homeless campsite. Same day.

ACT I

SCENE 1

Setting: Wal-Mart Store, people seen coming and going, the greeter stands by offering shopping carts to incoming shoppers.

JOE: (*Speaks while offering shopping carts to incoming shoppers.*) I am nobody, I know I'm nobody because the whole world tells me that I'm nobody, and it's the world in which I live, that same world that I hate to live in, but must. As I nod at the man dressed in a suit who I know is a professional man, I push the shopping cart towards him and he nods at me and grabs the handle, pushing it onto the shopping floor of Walmart. I know I am nobody because he only nodded back at me so I would let go of the shopping cart and he could get on with his shopping. They do it to me all day long, and he is a busy man, and I am but a 67-year former janitor who never got the benefit of a pension and must live on a monthly social security check of $650. My name is Joe.

SCENE 2

Setting: Front of Walmart

RICHARD: (*Speaks while people pass him by, walking into Walmart.*) I know they see me because I have eyes also, and I watch theirs as they flick back straight forward and walk right by me and pretend that I'm not there. I can't help it that I'm in a wheelchair or that I'm paralyzed from the waist down; it happened to me when I was in a car accident, just after I got back from Vietnam in 1971, and they made me into nobody when they said that I would have to rid myself of everything I owned, so that I could qualify to receive money from the federal government, specifically Medicaid. And, for the past 40 years I have felt like, and I have been, nobody. I only sit here outside of Walmart because my checks haven't come in for the past two months, and I'm broke, you understand, I'm broke, and so I'm just forced to sit here, in my wheelchair, and beg, but I don't mind because, after all, I can't really do much else and sometimes people engage me in conversation, which I like to talk to people but, of course, they must hurry on because they have lives and are busy and, well, I know who I am, in this world, I am nobody. My name is Richard.

SCENE 3

Setting: An office.

MOLLY: (*Speaks inside office while sweeping and cleaning.*) I know they see me but they pretend not to, especially when they walk past me when they leave their offices in the afternoon when I am just coming in to work, because they know that I am just going to clean their desks, vacuum and mop their floors and scrub and clean their sinks and toilets. I know they think I am nobody, and I used to think I was nobody too but I am starting to think differently because I have been starting to read a certain book and, in this book, it tells me that I am somebody and that it is, actually, those who are self-serving and selfish and greedy who are the ones who are guilty of not doing what is right and it makes me feel good; well, for awhile anyway, until I have to go to work and I see how people look at me and treat me: as if it pains them to even talk to me because, after all, I am only the cleaning lady, I am nobody (to them.) My name is Molly.

SCENE 4

Setting: A vineyard.

JUAN: (*Speaks while picking fruit.*) I live in New York in the summer and Florida in the winter but not because I am a wealthy man—no, in fact, I am very poor, and I don't really live in New York or Florida; I just stay in those states, just like I stay in Virginia, North Carolina, Pennsylvania, Georgia, Texas and California, and always in the picking seasons, because I make my living picking fruit from the orchards and farms. I don't speak very good English but I am learning because, someday, I wish to be somebody, so I am going to school. I know everyone thinks I am nobody, and I know I am nobody, for now, too. My name is Juan.

SCENE 5

Setting: Inside a casino.

RUSSELL RED CLOUD: (*Speaks while sweeping up cigarette butts in a gambling casino.*) I know what they think because I can see it in their eyes, as they walk past me, they know who I am, and they tell me with their looks of pity and some with their looks of contempt, as they hurry by me on their way to gambling away their paychecks or their mortgage money or their vacation money, in the casino. They know they are somebody because they have on suits and expensive leisure clothes, and they have wallets packed with green bills with pictures of dead presidents and statesmen on them and various plastic credit cards and identification cards, driver's licenses and military I.D. cards and other identification cards that identify them as somebody, while I mope along in my utility clothes with a small portable dustpan in one hand and a hand-held broom in the other, sweeping up the cigarette butts and refuse that litter the expansive tile floors that lead into the casino's gambling halls and eateries. I know they see that I am nobody, because I see it too, every time I pass by a mirror or go inside the bathroom that I must clean, but I don't care because I have my peace at night, after I clock out: I have my small room, and I have my bottle, and it makes me feel, at least for that short time period, like I am somebody even though I know I am nobody. My name is Russell Red Cloud.

SCENE 6

Setting: Inside a jail-cell.

BOBBY SYKES aka SHAKES: (*Speaks from inside a jail-cell.*) I am nobody, and I know it because I have been inside this jail cell for the past three months and nobody even comes to visit me, and I have to watch as the other prisoners have visits from their friends and families and lawyers. I've only had one visit in all this time, from the public defender, and he told me that if I plead out, plead guilty, that I would only get a year in the county jail, with credit for time served, which would mean I'd be out in nine more months. The biggest problem I have, with pleading guilty, is that I didn't do anything, see. I was just in the Quik-Chek store when the cops got there, and the clerk identified me as being one of the three hold-up men, and I didn't even know what he was talking about. Some of the other prisoners tell me to take the deal but to make sure I get a guarantee that the judge will actually give me the nine months and not nine years, and I'm really confused as to what to do. My street name is Shakes because I always used to shake a lot whenever I was scared but now I don't shake anymore.

I guess it's because I was scared all the time and, well, you can't just shake all the time, and so my body must have, like adjusted, know what I'm sayin'? Now I just go by my given name, Bobby Sykes.

SCENE 7

Setting: Man begging on a street-corner.

PETE: (*Speaks while he is begging on a street corner.*) I am nobody to just about everybody, I know that, and I know they appear to not even wish to touch me, even when they hand me some money. I don't understand why they appear afraid to touch me because I am not dirty, actually, quite the contrary, I take two showers a day, and on really hot days I go inside McDonalds or Wal-Mart and wash my face and hands and sometimes I eat breakfast or lunch, depending on how the day has gone. I've been a beggar for seven months now. I have an established corner here at an intersection on Highway 19, just in front of a Wal-Mart Shopping mall. A lot of cars and trucks go by this corner, and there is a 4-way traffic light at the intersection where I beg. I usually beg from six in the morning until noon and then take a break to eat something. Then I go back and beg until it either gets too hot to continue or until I have enough money to eat on for that day. I don't want to be a beggar; it's just that I lost my job and construction is all that I know. I was a laborer for four years straight, and then a contractor I was working for offered to hire me as an apprentice carpenter, and I worked for him for five years and got up to $25 an hour, which is top pay for a carpenter in South Florida. Anyway, things went so bad that the contractor I was working for went bankrupt, and I didn't even get my last two weeks' worth of wages, two grand I lost. Well, I had a wife and two little boys; Adam was, I mean, is, four and Petey is six. We lived in a really nice house just a couple blocks from the beach but we lost it when I couldn't make the mortgage payments of $1700 a month. My wife was working at Walmart and the family was together, but after all the creditors started calling her nonstop at work and at home, she had a nervous breakdown and one day just after I had started begging I came home to an empty house. My wife left a note for me, she had gone back to her mother's house in upstate New York and had taken the kids with her. I lived in my house until they padlocked it, and the cops said they'd arrest me if they caught me there. Sometimes I sneak back in and get a night's sleep but I heard that an investor just bought it, and there's a 4-rent sign in the front yard so I don't go back anymore but sometimes I get in other foreclosed houses that are empty and sometimes, when I get enough money, I sleep in a motel room where it only costs $25 bucks a night. I filed for unemployment insurance but my employer hadn't been paying his taxes for the last two years and so I was stuck. A lady at the employment office told me that I should go and see a lawyer but they all wanted money up front and I don't have any. I really miss my kids, and I try not to cry but sometimes I can't stop it from happening. The cops are the only ones who ever seem to really talk to me, and there's one guy who's really a great guy but most of them just hassle me and try to tell me to leave or they'll arrest me. A preacher stopped and gave me ten bucks the other day, a real good day for me and he invited me to his church, and I'm thinking of going, he left a little bible with me, and I've been reading it. At first it didn't make any sense to me, maybe because my parents never really took me to church, but lately I been looking in the New Testament, and I'm starting to think I might have a chance now. I think I'm even starting to think I might have a chance to be somebody again but I know, in this life, without money, who I am, I am nobody and so I do everything I can to get money. I bought two lottery tickets yesterday and I dream what would happen if one of them is a winner because I would win two hundred million dollars, can you imagine if I won? Man, I'd be more than just somebody and overnight too. My name is Pete.

SCENE 8

Setting: Food store.

DONNA: (*Speaks while shopping in a store with her baby.*) I feel like I'm nobody, and it really feels bad because I used to be somebody. I used to work at the Dollar Store, I was an assistant manager, and I think I could have become a manager. I also got my high school GED, and then I got a six-month dental school diploma so I could work as a dental assistant. What happened was my boyfriend made me pregnant, and he promised he would marry me but he never did, and then I had my baby, and he came around, and he gave me some money every week but then when he missed a week and then started giving me excuses and I took him to court he stopped paying me altogether, and now I really have bad feelings about this life and this world. I am lucky because my parents own two houses, and they let me live in one of them but they have a mortgage on it, and I can't pay it so they might have to rent it, and then I'll have to move in with them. I love my baby, and I want to go back to work so I can stay in my parents' house and help them pay the mortgage and work again but it just seems, sometimes, just so overwhelming. I have to use food stamps to get food and WIC coupons and it makes me feel like a second-class citizen, as the cashiers and managers in the food-stores give me their superior looks, especially when they make me pay cash for items they claim are *"not allowed"* on *"government assistance."* If only my boyfriend would marry me or help me out but he doesn't seem to care anymore. I cry a lot and feel lost. I go to church with my parents now and sometimes it makes me feel better but then my troubles come back, and I feel bad again because of the way everybody treats me when they realize I have no money: they see I am nobody. My name is Donna.

SCENE 9

ROGER: (*Speaks from inside a church.*) I am nobody, and it really feels terrible because I know, everybody knows, that I used to be somebody. I mean I was a millionaire, really, I was, I was a licensed general contractor, and the building boom in 2005 saw my company do so much business that I opened several other businesses, including a chain of Italian restaurants and a temporary labor pool chain that spread to 22 states. Then it all collapsed, and I was forced into bankruptcy. U.S. marshals even seized all my financial records, and I owe over five million dollars, according to them, to so many creditors I've lost count and track of them. I was considering suicide for a long time but then I got a visit from a friend of mine, a deacon in my church, and I began attending church again, and I feel better again, well, most of the time anyway. I used to give away hundreds of thousands of dollars to politicians, we bought them, but now the only money I ever give away is to a beggar every once in awhile, and I put some in the plate at church, I'm aware of my soul now and, as far as the beggars go I know how they feel; just like I do, they feel like they are nobody, and they're right, because we are, to this world. My name is Roger.

SCENE 10

NOBODY: (*One of three homeless Vietnam vets, speaks from homeless campsite, while cops roust them from their tents.*) I'm nobody, and I know I am, and the cops they know I am too. They came around our camp just yesterday and now it's gone. We, me and three other Vietnam vets, were living in a hobo camp. We had three large tents, and we always kept a fire going to scare off any raccoons and snakes. Anyway, a local murder brought cops into our camp, and they just about ruined it: they tore our tents apart and kicked the well-placed stones we had been making our campfires in, and they gave us the third-degree about the identity of the murder victim, and all because he was also a Vietnam veteran, as if we knew every Vietnam vet in the State of Florida. Well, anyway, they questioned all my buddies, and they all told the cops that they didn't know who the guy was when they showed them the pictures of him. I was the last one to be interrogated, and I looked at the pictures, they had six of them, very carefully, they all showed pictures of a man in his 60s who was dressed in rags, with a long white-speckled beard, but then one of them showed a picture of a man in a navy uniform; it looked like he had been a Chief Petty Officer, and it was hard to compare him with the other pictures. I had never seen the guy before, but as I handed the pictures back to the cop he growled at me.

COP: You know who he was?

(*Pause*)

NOBODY: Yeah, I know who he was,

(*Pause*)

COP: (*Glares at me the homeless Vietnam vet.*) C'mon wise-guy?

(*Pause*)

HOMELESS VIETNAM VET: (*Glances at his three homeless Vietnam vet friends.*) He was one of us.

(*Pause*)

COP: C'mon wiseguy; what ayah mean by *one of us?*

(*Pause*)

HOMELESS VIETNAM VET: He was nobody, officer, just like us, he was nobody!

MR. PAYBACK

AN ORIGINAL PLAY IN ONE ACT

THIS PLAY TAKES PLACE IN FT. LAUDERDALE IN 1986.

CHARACTERS:

BILLY CARTER aka BAM-BOOM: Age 20
MICHAEL JOHNSON aka SONNY: Age 21
SCOTT SANDS: COMEDY CLUB EMCEE Age 25-35
JOE FARLEY: AUDIENCE MEMBER Age 25-35
VIRGINIA FARLEY: JOE'S WIFE Age 25-35
KENNY J. KIDDING aka MR. PAYBACK: Age 25-35
BILL EPSTEIN: Age 55-65
BOBBY GREENE: Age 25-35
DETECTIVE SGT. PAUL RAYMOND: Age35-45
LT. KEITH KEREMSKY: Age 45-55
AUDIENCE: 10-15

SCENE 1: Dark night, 8:30 PM, Saturday evening, Ft. Lauderdale. Police chase Bam-Boom and Sonny.

SCENE 2: Inside Comedy Club, where Bam-Boom & Sonny seek refuge.

SCENE 3: Foyer in front anteroom to Comedy Club.

SCENE 4: Comedy Club after gun battle between Bam-Boom, Sonny and the police.

ACT I
SCENE 1

Setting: Bam-Boom and Sonny are in their brand-new 1986 black corvette, being chased by the police, the sirens are blasting. (*We see the driver and passenger on center stage, with the rest being sound effects and dialogue between the two men in the corvette.*) Bam-Boom is a 20-year-old high school dropout. He is also the chairman of the board of a thriving business that deals crack cocaine. Bam-Boom runs everything from manufacturing the product to distribution and sales, via the street. He 'owns' almost an entire neighborhood in Northwest Fort Lauderdale and is an American success story. Bam-Boom, in typical American tradition, lets everyone, himself included, see how much of a success he is, as he drives the newest cars, wears solid gold jewelry and takes no backtalk from anyone. He has worked his way up from the mean streets the only way he knew how, through violence and intimidation, and has earned his street-name by hitting (bam) and then shooting (boom) his competitors until they either moved to another territory or he killed them. His favorite weapon is a .357 Magnum and he uses it at even the slightest hint of treachery or disrespect. He uses the weapon exactly as the manufacturer had intended it to be used, to kill people be those people gang members, friends, partners or a policeman attempting to arrest him, as is now the case.

BAM-BOOM: (*Glances at his wrist-watch, sees it's 8:25 PM, as the corvette approaches 140 mph and the patrol car is almost out of sight in his rear-view mirror, when Michael 'Sonny' Johnson, Bam-Boom's home-boy and partner in crime, sitting next to him*

tells him to slow down.) Yeh-yeh, I got it Sonny, I got it.
SONNY: Hang a rye on Thiree-firs', man, **NOW!**
BAM-BOOM: (*Slows to 80 mph and turns the steering wheel hard to the right, as the corvette roars down Northwest 31st Avenue, which turns into Martin Luther King Jr. Boulevard when Bam-Boom curses his luck; he had picked the corvette up that very afternoon and had yet to have one of his police-band radios installed. He puts the pedal to the metal.*) Damn they usin' dah horn Sonny, too bad we din' get one in here yet.
SONNY: Slow down Bee and makes ah left on Fed-ill, **NOW!**
BAM-BOOM: (*Turns the wheel sharply to the left and the Chevy careens out of control, skidding into an alley and ramming into a multitude of wooden crates and cardboard boxes. Sounds effects and a black-out then the stage lightens to show Bam-Boom and Sonny Johnson have crashed and are momentarily stunned but soon realize they have crashed into a large number of grocery store boxes and crates and were completely hidden from view. Bam-Boom smiles at his partner, who returns the glance ten-fold —as a faraway siren echoes in the distance.*) We inna clear Sonny-boy, less get outta here.

SCENE 2

Setting: A Comedy Club, just around the corner from where Bam-Boom has crashed the corvette.

EMCEE: Good evening, Ladies and gentlemen, I'm Scott Sands, your emcee tonight. (*Nods at the audience, and smiles at a young couple, sitting close to the stage*) And your name is?

AUDIENCE COUPLE: (*Exchanging bemused glances.*) Oh, I'm Joe and this is my wife Virginia.
EMCEE: Joe and Virginia and where are y'all from?
JOE: Oh-ah, er right here. We're from here, right here.
EMCEE: I see ... so you sleep on the floor here, do you? (*Audience laughs heartily and the emcee glances at a man sitting at a corner table, a young up and coming comedian, one who always went for the jugular. He was said to be more aggressively insulting than even Don Rickles but Rickles was a known commodity, a star, whereas this comedian was relatively unknown and finding it ever increasingly hard to get bookings. The emcee, realizes the audience can't begin to fathom the degree of insults that they were about to be subjected to and he wasn't about to forewarn them. He smiles at the local couple.*) Of course I'm just kidding, sir, you know that? (*Glances sideways and sees the acidic comedian's scowl easily. He had inadvertently but purposely stolen the comic's opening line. Realizing he couldn't prepare the audience for the coming onslaught anyway, he smiles.*) So, I'm Scott Sands, and now, ladies and gentlemen, strap on your seat-belts. The next act comes out with both guns blazing, as you'll soon see. So, here he is, off-the-wall, from a distant planet, known far and short, near and wide, as Mister Payback, and yule soon understand why kiddies, here he is, Kenny Jay Kidding, **MISTER PAYBACK!** (*Sands offers his hand to Kidding, who proffers his only to jerk it backwards at the last second, his thumb shaking next to his ear, in the wind, his first laugh, at the emcee's expense and one he couldn't retaliate on, as the stage was no longer his but now belonged to the one who was in possession of the microphone, but only for as long as he could keep control of it. Kidding jerks the microphone from the stand and walks towards the audience. He stands at the edge of the stage.*) My name is Kenny J. Kidding, dah Jay stands for Justin but we shortened it to

Just when I-us just a kid and I been just kiddin' ever since, so don't take nuttin' I say personally. Yeah, I was born in New York but I grew up all ovah the country, actually all ovah the world, see my father was in the Navy, yeah New York, San Antonio, Guam, dah Phil-ah-peens, Jaypan, Okee-nah-wah, but most ah my life I grew up in a small African nation. Yeah. Maybe yah heard of it, Washington Dee-Cee? (*The audience laughs heartily and the comic smiles crookedly. They were a good crowd, so far. He strolls to the young couple at ringside and smiles deceptively.*) So, Virgin which room is yours? I mean, bein' as you live here? (*The audience laughs but the girl blushes.*)

VIRGINIA: No, you see, well we're from here, I mean we're from Fort—actually oh, oh ...

MR. PAYBACK: You're from actually, oh? Actually, Ohio, is that it? You're from Actually, Ohio?

(*Beat*)

VIRGINIA: (*Audience laughs heartily but the woman keeps on providing straight-lines anyway.*) Well, you see we came down here from Virgin-yah and then we, see, we first came down about a year ago, and see, well we liked it so ...

MR. PAYBACK: (*The crowd is giggling slightly, when the comic whips the microphone away from the woman's mouth.*) Gee-zuz, *WOMEN!* Takes 'em a year tah learn how tah talk then fifty tah learn how tah shut up. (*Roaring laughter and Mr. Payback continues his assault.*) Well, Virgin where are you from, I mean originally?

(*Beat*)

JOE: She's from ... we're from Virginia and her name is also Virginia, not virgin ... even though she is one or-er, she wah ... ah ... us. I mean ... (*The audience is laughing shallowly.*)

MR. PAYBACK: (*Looking at Virginia.*) This is *your* husband?

VIRGINIA: Well we are from Virginia and ...

MR. PAYBACK: Ah-hah. Virgin from Virginia. (*Looks at audience.*) Sounds like a movie title. The Virgin from Virginia. (*Audience is laughing and Joe is scowling. Mr. Payback looks at Joe, then at Virginia.*) I gotta tell you Virgin, oh, sorry, just kiddin', you know, Virginia, Virginia from Virginia, you could ah done better really, I mean, let's face it Joe is one ugly suckah. (*Audience laughs loudly as Joe tries to smile but can't. Looks at audience.*) Remember what Adam said to Eve, don't yah? (*Looking at Virginia, then the audience*) Said stand back, there's no tellin' how big this thing's gonna get? (*Audience roars and, after nearly a full-minute of laughter, just as the laughter dies down, he looks at an unsmiling Joe and nods towards him.*) Wait a minute, Joe ain't got it … yet! (*Laughter rises an octave*) Yeah, Virgin-ayah you could ah done a lot better'n diz go-rilla. (*Turns to the audience*) Ain't he ugly?
(*Beat*)
VIRGINIA: (*Looking up at Mr. Payback.*) Well, are you available? (*Crowd erupts in boisterous laughter.*)
MR. PAYBACK: (*Looks at Virginia, who is smiling, and then Joe, who looks mad.*) Ah, no, Virgin from Virginia, not me man, no heh-heh, I'm married. Yeah, gottah wife and four kids with a fifth one on the way. Yup, my wife came home from the pediatrician just the other night with a big smile on ah face. I says what's with you? She says, dah pediatrician says I have the breasts of an eighteen-yeah old. (*He pauses, looking at audience.*) Heh! Yeah, I says to her, what'd he say about yah thirty-three year old ass? (*Audience roars and Mr. Payback smiles and waits until the laughter has died down considerably.*) Yeah, so then she says he didn't say nuttin' 'bout you, he didn't mention *you* at all, left you outta the whole conversation. (*Roaring laughter from the audience and Joe laughs with them, as Mr. Payback, who has done the routine innumerable times, knew he would, but Mr.*

Payback is not done yet and when he grins at Virginia you could barely see his teeth: if you looked closely you would swear he looked like a lion moving in for the kill, as his long brown hair quivers, when he swivels his head towards Virginia.) But, if my wife evah gets sick, heh-heh I'd like tah give yah a call. (*Audience roars with laughter again, seeing Joe scowl and shake his head, yet again and Mr. Payback raises his eyebrows ala Groucho Marx at the audience and then Virginia.*) Yeah Virgin ...Virgin-nah-yah, we work things out right she could be *dead* in about two or three hours. (*Audience laughter and Mr. Payback notices that a heavyset man, sitting in the corner just in front of the stage, has just placed his feet up on the stage, using the stage for a foot-rest causing Mr. Payback to walk over to him and look down, directly at his legs propped on the stage.*) Boy, diz guy wants tah get in show biz so bad he can't even keep his feet off the stage.
HEAVY-SET MAN: Yeah, I wanna get a foot up on yah, ahah-rah, ah-rarha, ahah, a foot up on yah, hah!
MR. PAYBACK: (*Sees Joe laughing now at what the heavy-set man has said to Mr. Payback when the crowd laughs.*) What'd you just come from the Mort Downey show? You put your shoes on backwards, you're bumping into yourself. Man, if your I.Q. was a point higher, you'd be a baloney sandwich. (*Crowd roars with laughter now and the heavy-set man stands up and fidgets with his crotch, then heads towards the side aisle, towards the bathroom.*) Will all homosexuals please stand up, and go to your favorite of all places, the little boy's room? (*Audience roars with laughter again but becomes almost silent, when Mr. Payback, walks back to where Joe and Virginia are sitting and laughing. He stares down at them and smiles.*) Thought I wuz done with yah huh Joe? (*As Mr. Payback attacks the crowd further, Bill Epstein, the club's owner, frowns, wondering whether he should book him again, he was funny, no question, but why take a chance he would insult a*

customer and scare away business? Epstein had seen most of the local acts and knew that he was in a position to pick and choose from a very large number of them. On open-mic night, they always had too many comic's wanting to come and do their act, if they even had an act; many of them just trying to get one together but he didn't have to pay them. He smiles, despite himself, as Kenny J. Kidding attacks the couple sitting up-front and the audience roars with laughter. He strolls out, into the foyer of the club, thinking how it was always funny to the audience just as long as it wasn't them Mr. Payback was attacking.)

SCENE 3

Setting: Light fades on Mr. Payback as Epstein walks out into the foyer, just as two black youths run inside the club, both breathing heavily.

EPSTEIN: (*Nods at Bobby Greene, his doorman, who smiles.*) What?
GREENE: They just came in sir, I was just comin' outta the men's room and I just saw them sir.
EPSTEIN: (*Waves Greene off.*) No problem Bobby, Take care of these gentlemen while I use the men's room myself.
GREENE: What can I do for you gentlemen?
BAM-BOOM: We wanna watch chew show man?
GREENE: I'm sorry but I'll need to see some eye-dee and there's still a five-dollar cover-charge and a two-drink minimum?
BAM-BOOM: (*Eyeballs Sonny and then Greene and pulls out a*

roll of bills as thick as his fist; peels off a hundred-dollar bill.) Keep it man.
GREENE: (*Looks woefully at the bathroom door that has just closed on Epstein.*) Just a minute, fellas. (*Walks to cash-register and grabs two tickets.*) Here yah go, gentlemen, sit wherever you wish.
BAM-BOOM: (*Smiles, winks at Sonny.*) Yeah, we do dat, Homes.
MR. PAYBACK: (*Sees Bam-Boom and Sonny Johnson walking in, as a waitress approaches their table, in the center of the room.*) Ah-hah, new meat. Come right in, gents. Hey, take a seat up front here so I kin get on yah case. (*Bam-Boom nods at Johnson, who whispers something to him, as they talk in low monotones and Mr. Payback walks off the stage and up to their table, smiling at the audience, many of whom are already laughing.*) Say man, haven't I seen your picture on a post office wall? (*Crowd laughs but Bam-Boom simply glares at the comedian, who smiles at him.*) Is that your nose? Damn man and I thought you had a banana in yah mouth? (*Crowd roars, seeing Bam-Boom's broken nose and his gangster-style dress and the anger on his face.*) Man-oh-man, that thing is suckin' up the sand. (*Turns towards the audience and nods his head at Bam-Boom.*) Take diz guy tah the beach he could clear a landin' zone fah a helicopter. Yeah, c'mon ovah here and breathe. Heh-heh, just kiddin' my man, really, I am. (*Audience is laughing heartily and Mr. Payback makes believe he is walking back to the stage, then turns and puts his face within inches of Bam-Boom's, as if he was further studying his facial features.*) Guy's got his own portable vacuum cleaner here. Hey man, kin I give yah a ride home, I need the carpets in my car cleaned. (*Audience roars as Bam-Boom reaches for his piece but Johnson kicks him on the shin as the comic walks away from them.*)
SONNY: Be cool Bee, man, dude's jus' playin' wid jah.
BAM-BOOM: Man, diz punk muhfuh ...

MR. PAYBACK: (*Realizes the audience hears the two men talking to each other but can't hear what they are saying and throws out a line.*) Lookit man, they matchin' wits wid each other, hah, yeah a half-wit wid a dim-wit. (*Audience responds heartily as a booming laughter resounds throughout the small room and Mr. Payback knows 100% of them are laughing. Both young gangsters have shaved, bald heads and, as the glistening bald domes move towards each other when Sonny Johnson counsels Bam-Boom to keep his cool, Mr. Payback nods towards them.*) Will yah look at the light shinin' on those two beach-balls. I thought for a second there somebody's was tryin' tah **MOON** me!" (*The audience roared as loud as they ever had, throughout the night, and Bam-Boom's angry retort was lost in the laughter and commotion. When it finally died down Mr. Payback continued his relentless attack.*) Man, when God made you he was obviously suffering from a quality control problem. (*Laughter*) Next time you donate your clothes to the Salvation Army do us all a favor and stay in 'em. You should donate your brain to medical science, man, with the gas prices like they are we could use it for fuel, yeah, we'll call it ass-ah-haul.(*Mr. Payback sees a policeman in the back of the club, just entering the room. He smiles craftily and nods towards the back of the club.*) Officer, well, Come right in. I've been up here on stage now, (*Glances at his watch.*) for a good three and a half hours. (*Audience roars again, seeing the cop.*) Please, believe me, and just because my car's full of tee-vees and stereo's don't mean I know anythin' about how they got there. (*Audience is laughing as is Mr. Payback himself when the first shot rings out. Sonny Johnson had a .38 Smith in his hand and a plain-clothes Broward County detective falls to the floor. That was when all hell broke loose and bullets flew like ping-pong balls in the Chinese Olympics. People were running around like rats in a lion's cage. All together, six people would pay a visit to the county* coroner's office that evening, four policemen, one ghetto drug peddler and one up and coming comedian. Billy 'Bam-Boom' Carter had five bullets lodged in his body but would recover enough to spend the remainder of his life in prison or die in Florida's electric chair. Light fades away, goes dark.)

SCENE 4

Setting: Comedy Club; Chairs and tables are strewn around and blood covers a great deal of the area, much of it taped off.

DETECTIVE SGT. PAUL RAYMOND: (*Smiles at Virginia.*) So, he shot this comedian at point-blank range, while the other kid shot at the policemen?
VIRGINIA: That's what I saw, sir.
(*Beat*)
RAYMOND: (*Shuts off his tape recorder, shakes Joe and Virginia Farley's hands.*) Thank you very much Mr. and Mrs. Farley, we thank you very much for your time. You don't know how lucky you are to have not been injured?
JOE: Oh yes we do, sir. Can we go now?
(*Beat*)
RAYMOND: Sure, no problem, we may need you to testify if Mr. Carter lives.
(*Beat*)
JOE: Well, we'll see about that sir.
LT. KEITH KEREMSKY: (*Has just walked up to his partner after interviewing a half-dozen eye-witnesses.*) Ah, Mr. Farley, could I ask you one question please sir, before you leave.
JOE: Sure, what is it?
KEREMSKY: Well, our witnesses seem to have seen Bam-Boom,

ah Mr. Billy Carter shoot this comedian point-blank and we're trying to figure out why he …
JOE: I'll tell you why; he insulted the man, made fun of him, turned him into a fool, that's why. He beat him into the ground.
(*Beat*)
KEREMSKY: (*Holds his hand up in the air, signaling for Joe to stop talking.*) Whoa ah, ah, are you saying that he *verbally* beat this kid up? By *insulting* him?
JOE: That's right; that's exactly what I'm saying, sir.
KEREMSKY: You sound like he may have insulted you tonight?
(*Beat*)
VIRGINIA: (*Joe opens his mouth to speak but Virginia interrupts him.*) He insulted practically everyone in the room tonight officer.
JOE: Can we go now?
KEREMSKY: Certainly sir, you may leave and thank you very much.
(*Beat*)
JOE: (Grabs his wife's elbow and steers her up the aisle.)
RAYMOND: This guy was an insult comedian Keith. I seen him once myself; me and three other guys at a comedy club in Lauderdale at the Day's Inn. He was the emcee.
KEREMSKY: Was he …
RAYMOND: The guy was brutal, he insulted half the people in the audience but damn the guy was funny. Mister Payback, shhh, the guy could match words wid anybody, put Graham six feet under and it was hilarious, you shouldah been there.
KEREMSKY: Shee-it, Johnny Graham Cracker? Nobody ever …
RAYMOND: Keith, this guy would put Don Rickles to shame, he was brutal. Graham Cracker was ready to crawl in a hole.
(*Beat*)
KEREMSKY: This guy give him a chance to respond? To …
RAYMOND: Keith, he gave Graham Cracker the Mike. Put it

right in his hand.
KEREMSKY: Never heard ah that before; he musta been good?
RAYMOND: Oh hell, he was funny. I practically broke a rib laughin' at this guy.
KEREMSKY: Too bad huh?
RAYMOND: You mean about him gettin' shot and killed?
KEREMSKY: Yeah. What the fugg's the world comin' to anyway Paulie, y'know? I could see this in Russia but here. Words, the guy gets killed over words?
RAYMOND: (*Looks at the blood and torn-apart room.*) Yeah.
KEREMSKY: I got thirty in next month.
RAYMOND: You gonna pack it in Keith?
(*Beat*)
KEREMSKY: I think so Paulie. Bam-Boom shot this guy before anybody else? I mean even though our guys were firin' on 'im? That's how *nuts he is over words*?
RAYMOND: Must be Keith. I mean, he's got five slugs in 'im, don't he? Billy Carter used to run track at Dillard. Did the hundred in under ten seconds. I remember him he was on the track team with my son and look at how he turned out? A muh-fuh drug dealer and murderer at age twenty?
(*Beat*)
KEREMSKY: If he lives I'm gonna see he gets the chair, one way or the other?
RAYMOND: Thought you'us gonna retire Keith?
KEREMSKY: I can still testify, can't I?
RAYMOND: Yeah, let's go get some chow Keith.
KEREMSKY: (Stubs out a cigarette.) Sounds good, partner, sounds good.

CURTAIN END OF PLAY

THE GUN

AN ORIGINAL PLAY IN TWO ACTS

THE SETTING OF THIS PLAY IS ATLANTA, IN 1999.
CHARACTERS:

MAURICE JOHNSON aka MOJO: Age 30-40
GUN DEALER: AGE 25-35
PICKUP TRUCK DRIVER: AGE 25-35
ABEL JAMMES aka A.J.: AGE 19
JEROME MILLER aka SUGARMAN: AGE 19
MARSHA: AGE 19
SAL JONES aka WEST-END SALLY: AGE 66
BOBBY McLAINE aka SKEETER AGE 10
CLARENCE JACKSON aka SNAP AGE 10

ACT I

MOJO BUYS A GUN FROM AN UNLICENSED VENDOR, WHO DID NO BACKGROUND CHECKS AND SOLD IT AS IS, FOR CASH. THE PISTOL IS AN ISRAELI 9MM WITH NO SERIAL # & UNTRACEABLE. MOJO SHOOTS AND KILLS A MAN OVER A PARKING SPOT AND THROWS GUN IN AN ALLEY, WHERE IT IS PICKED UP BY A.J. WHO SHOOTS AND KILLS A CONVEINENCE STORE CLERK. HE THROWS THE GUN IN AN ALLEYWAY.

ACT I   SCENES & SETTINGS

SCENE 1: Setting: Farmer's Market, Atlanta, GA.
SCENE 2: Setting: Apartment in Buckhead.
SCENE 3: Setting: Alley where Mojo threw gun.
SCENE 4: Setting: A.J. and Marsghas's apartment.

ACT 2

ACT II   SCENES & SETTINGS

SKEETER AND SNAP, WALKING DOWN AN ALLEYWAY SHORTCUT TO THEIR ELEMENTARY SCHOOL COME UPON THE DISCARDED PISTOL. SNAP PICKS IT UP AND, MISTAKENLY, SHOOTS & KILLS HIS NEIGHBOR AND BEST FRIEND SKEETER.

SCENE 1: Setting: Discount gas station.
SCENE 2: Setting: Projects.
SCENE 3: Setting: West-end Sally's house.
SCENE 4: Alleyway in Projects.

ACT I

SCENE 1

Setting: A Farmer's Market in Greater Atlanta Metro District

MOJO: (*Walks into a tent where an arsenal of rifles and guns are on tables for sale. Looks over the pistols, picks one up.*) Nice-lookin' gun.
GUN DEALER: That be a good pick too. Jericho 941, a nine millimeter, eight rounds innah clip and one innah chamber. Come wif two clips too, eight in a clip and one innah chamber, gib yah sementeen shots know uhm sayin'?
(*Beat*)
MOJO: (*Relinquishes pistol to dealer, who shoves a clip into the bottom of the grip and smiles.*) Two clips huh?
GUN DEALER: Yeh, like I said eight inna clip and one inna chamber, you gon' get off sementeen shots in no time, know uhm sayin'? Lightweight, only two and a quarter pound. An Israeli gun, bruddah, dah bes' know uhm sayin'? Come wif a boss holster too bruddah, know uhm sayin'?
MOJO: How much you wants fo' it?
(*Beat*)
GUN DEALER: Six bucks Blood, know uhm sayin'
MOJO: Yo gone needs eye-dee'un taxes, all dat shee-it?
GUN DEALER: Shee-it Homes, I'm free-lance, jus' six man.
(*Beat*)
MOJO: No registration?
GUN DEALER: I said I'm free-lance bro'ah, know uhm sayin'?

MOJO: I give yah five, cash.

GUN DEALER: Five and a half and you gots it Blood, know uhm sayin'?

(*Beat*)

MOJO: (*Pulls out a wad of bills, peals off six bills.*) Got fifty?

GUN DEALER: Auno. (*Looks in his shoe-box cash register.*) Yeh, I gots it, here yo is Blood. (*Hands Mojo two twenties and a ten.*) Come back anytime bro-ah, know uhm sayin'?

MOJO: Yo man, I knows you from Decatur?

(*Beat*)

GUN DEALER: Maybe bro; I lived dere fo' a cupoh years, know uhm sayin'?

MOJO: I seen you off Candler Road din' I? By dah high school?

GUN DEALER: Auno, maybe. I bees ovah dere once-tin-while, know uhm sayin'?

MOJO: (*They bang fists.*) See yo roun' niggah.

GUN DEALER: Yeh niggah, is all good, know uhm sayin'?

SCENE 2

Setting: An apartment in Buckhead, a ritzy section of Atlanta where MoJo maintains an apartment by selling cars at a used car lot and drugs at a substantial markup. MoJo served two years of a five year sentence for selling crack cocaine and is currently on probation.

MOJO: (*On a big-screen T.V., President Clinton is condemning the shootings at Heritage High School in Littleton, Colorado and is seq-waying into his praise of the successful bombing mission in Kosovo, as MoJo pours himself another shot of whiskey from a* *bottle into a glass and walks onto his porch, which provides a splendid view of Atlanta's polluted and congested streets. He lights a cigarette and inhales nicotine and polluted air, then glances down towards the street, where his shiny new Dodge Intrepid, parked just in front of his building, sits glistening in the early morning sun. Scowling, he notices a pickup truck pulling into a reserved space, just behind his, and hurries towards the door of his second floor studio apartment, pulling the .44 from its holster as he runs out his front door and down the hallway.)* Muhfuh in trouble wid me man, I sees what he wants. (*Sees the driver of an old, fender-damaged pickup truck, walking towards the building next to his*) Hey man get dat piece ah junk truck outta here man.

PICKUP TRUCK DRIVER: I lives here too, Jack!

(*Beat*)

MOJO: You lives at thirty-three hun'red man, who you kiddin'? I see you come and go man. Yo' can't find a parkin' space 'at yo' problem muhfuh. Get yo' own space, these is fo' thirty-two hun'red only and you knows it. And my name ain't Jack.

PICKUP TRUCK DRIVER: (*Walks towards MoJo.*) Shee-it, niggah, I puts a cap in yo' haid, don't shut yo' trap.

MOJO: (*Eyes narrow and his nostrils flare open, as he reaches for his piece.*) Muh-fuh, who yo' think you talkin' to?

(*Pause*)

PICKUP TRUCK DRIVER: I see yo' shit, Jack. (*Sees MoJo's piece and runs towards his truck and opens the passenger-side door, then opens the glove-box. He pulls out a .357 Magnum and turns towards MoJo when a slug from MoJo's .44 crashes through the rear widow of his 1988 Ford pick-up and then into his neck, splaying blood, splinters of bone, and slabs of skin onto the seat-covers, even as he raises his .357 and his truck's interior is splattered and splashed with meaty chunks of his brain matter and*

bits of bloody skull-bones, as MoJo fires three more slugs into the man's head. He walks over to the truck and sees the carnage his pistol has done and smiles, then kicks the man, who is dead.)
MOJO: Dumb-ass muhfuh, mess wid MoJo. (*He gets in his car and speeds away and quickly disappears. Light fades away. Lights up, we see MoJo in an alleyway where he throws his 9 mm pistol. Lights fade away.*)

SCENE 3

Setting: The same alley where MoJo threw the gun, two days later.

A.J.: (*Abel 'A.J.,' James picks up the .44 Magnum and dusts it off. It's lying in an alley, just behind a gaggle of garbage cans. James rubs it on his shirt. He smiles, as the chrome-plated gun glistens up at him and turns to childhood friend Jerome 'Sugarman' Miller*) Damn niggah, lookit diz, gots a clip wid shee-it, look like (*Examines clip.*) only three bullets left.
SUGARMAN: It gots a serial niggah?
A.J.: Naw-ah, sumbody filed it. (*He quickly stuffs it into his pants and smiles. Both youths had grown up in Herndon Homes, and were familiar with drugs and guns. They knew they could sell it and make some money, money that A.J. needed now that his girlfriend was pregnant. He had just gotten them an apartment uptown, away from all the harshness and violence of the inner city slums, which were spread throughout almost every direction in the greater Metropolitan Atlanta area.*) Man, I sell it Sugar; now I'm getting' wid Marsha and movin' cross town near Emory.
SUGARMAN: She goin' d'ah Emory now, ain't she A-Jay?
A.J.: Yeah and I'm workin' at the Deli over there it be nice niggah,

I gone stay away from here but gotta get my moms outta here too.
SUGARMAN: I hear you niggah, I wanna get outta 'ah Homes too man but wha' I'm 'onna do? Ain't got but nine-umph grade and can't pass dah Gee-E-Dee, took dat sucker three times too.
A.J.: Yeah, you get it niggah, maybe I sit in fo' you bro'ah.
(*Beat*)
SUGARMAN: At be good A.J. I could get wid some jobs mebbe if I had dat 'ploma man. You gone back now, wha'chew gone do wif diz nine? You know Dago Johnny pro'lee gib you fifty fo' it?
A.J.: Shee-it he ain't gone get it. Diz nine is gone get top dollah or I keep it awhile niggah. C'mon niggah, we gotta get back cross dah street, gotta say bye to my moms and sisters and take Marsha home. Here take diz and we call it mine.
(*Beat*)
SUGARMAN: (*Looks at the twenty-dollar bill and hands it back to A.J.*) C'mon niggah we is hangin' par-nahs, we is bruddahs since fo'evah. We be clean, yo' seed it firs' anyways niggah.
A.J.: (*Puts fist towards Sugarman, who bumps it.*) Less go niggah, Marsha gone be mad as it is.
SUGARMAN: She hate comin' back dah projects huh?
A.J.: Yeah man, wha'chew gone do man? Let's go I be back someday soon and we sell diz nine and split?
SUGARMAN: I see what Dago Johnny gone give you Blood, if ain't nuff we go to West-end Sally?
A.J.: Sound like a plan, niggah, we do it sometime soon. (*Pulls out the pistol and they walk away. Light fades to dark.*)

SCENE 4

Setting: A.J and Marsha's apartment.

A.J.: I gone get anovah job Marsh' I tol' jew dat, wha'chew wants?
MARSHA: Stop talkin' like you innah hood allah time A.J. I know you don't have to talk like that and so do you? And you're not going to go back to the projects again this afternoon. We need to stay away from there.
(*Beat*)
A.J.: How 'bout my moms and sisters?
MARSHA: How about them A.J.? I don't go and visit Skippy?
(*Beat*)
A.J.: Skippy only yo' cousin, yo family done aw'eady moved to Stockbridge in 'at big house they gots now and …
MARSHA: A.J. I'm not going with you tonight back to Herndon?
A.J.: (*Obviously mad, yells at her.*) You gotta go, you gone be married to me nex' month, ain't chew?
MARSHA: A.J. I love you but …
A.J.: Marsh' yo' gone have our son in three mo' months?
(*Pause*)
MARSHA: (*Starts to cry*) A.J. You have to change; you can get a degree too? Look, how easily you passed the G-E-D? You can …
A.J.: Damn Marsh' I ain't gone change ebree piece ah myse'f jus' as you say so. Auno what I'm do? I gotta see Sugar tonight we gots biz-nuz. I gots tah …
MARSHA: A.J. I swear I won't listen to that kinna talk. You need to stay away from the projects and you need to stay especially away from Sugarman.
A.J. (*Obviously mad, runs over to Marsha and raises his hand to slap her but stops himself.*) Sugar my homeboy, we bruddahs.
MARSHA: Go ahead and hit your six-months pregnant wife A.J. Go on, hit me?
(*Beat*)
A.J.: Damn Marsha I auno 'bout … shee-it, woman you can't run my muhfuh life. (*Goes dark.*)

ACT II

SCENE 1

Setting: Discount Gas Station.

A.J.: (*Pumping gas into his gas-tank he realizes he has only five dollars and he has pumped in ten gallons of gas at .88 a gallon and owes $8.80. He looks around, jumps inside his car and turns on the engine. He sees the East Indian gas attendant coming towards his car and reaches in his glove box, pulling out the 9mm pistol that he had put five more bullets in and now held eight in the clip and one in the chamber.*) Sup man?
ATTENDANT: Mahn, you have to pay for your gas?
A.J.: (*Points pistol at attendant.*) Jus' get back in yah station man.
ATTENDANT: (*Had been robbed once before and they had gotten away with it. The police found a pistol the robbers had dropped when they left and it was a starter pistol that only fired blanks. He grabs the barrel of the gun and pulls just enough for A.J.'s finger to push the trigger.*) You have to pay the ...
A.J.: BAM! (*Gun fires.*) Oh shit; hey, hey I didn't ... I didn't mean to ... (*Gets out of car and sees the attendant's body lying on the ground, blood seeping from his side.*) Hey, hey I din ... (*Sees three people staring at him and realizes he still has the gun in his hand. Jumps behind the wheel and pulls out. Light fades as we hear the car accelerating.*)

SCENE 2

Setting: A.J., in the projects; talking to Sugarman.

A.J: He was bleedin' pre' bad Sugar.
SUGARMAN: Wha'chew gone do wif dah Nine?
A.J. : Auno Sug'?
(*Beat*)
SUGARMAN: Less go see West-end Sally, niggah. Look, he right down ah stree'. (*Light fades.*)

SCENE 3

Setting: West-end Sally's house.

SUGARMAN: Wha'chew gib fo' diz nine Sal?
(*Beat*)
WEST-END SALLY: (*West-end Sally looks at pistol and sees the serial numbers are filed off.*) C-note.
SUGARMAN: Niggah, diz ah Israeli Nine, muhfuh is precise.
WEST-END SALLY: I'm aware of the make of the gun. It's hot.
(*Beat*)
SUGARMAN: Wha' dat gots to do wid it? We doin' targit pratiz?
WEST-END SALLY: It's hotter than that Sugar; diz piece may have shot somebody recently, in which case ... fifty bucks.
(*Beat*)
SUGARMAN: Fid-ee bugs, niggah auno, dat shee-it yo talkin'.
WEST-END SALLY: Twenty bucks now.
A.J.: Why you keep goin' down Sal?

WEST-END SALLY: You know why A.J., I tol you it's hot and *now I **know*** it is.

A.J.: I'll throw it inna lake before I take twenty.

(*Beat*)

WEST-END SALLY: I don't want it, you niggahs get outta here. (*Sugarman and A.J look around and see Sally's bodyguards, two monsters, both with nine millimeters strapped to their chests.*)

SUGARMAN: (*Looks at Sal Jones, a 66 year-old pimp, drug-dealer and buyer/seller of anything of value. He had almost total control of the west-end projects and anyone who crossed him was very likely to end up in the hospital or the morgue.*) Shee-it, less go A.J.(*They walk outside and hear sirens blasting. They start to run and Sugarman yells at A.J to throw the nine away, which he does in an alleyway.*)

SCENE 4

Setting: Alleyway in projects. A week later.

SKEETER: Man Snap, you shouldah seen Sylbestsah Strawown wif dah Sheen gun man, key-key-key-keyyow-chhhhcashooom. Snap let's go through dah alleyway, it be shorter?

(*Beat*)

SNAP: You know our moms don't want us goin' that way but okay, less go. (*Cuts over to the alleyway that leads directly to the boys' elementary school. Littered with garbage cans, bottles, condoms, drug paraphernalia and sometimes human bodies the boys hadn't walked ten steps before Snap sees the sun glistening off something behind a garbage can and walks over and picks it* *up.*)

SKEETER: Wha'chew gots Snapper?

(*Beat*)

SNAP: Snap holds it up and it shines in the sun. Is a gun Skeet. Lookee here man. (*Hands it to Skeeter.*)

SKEETER: Shee-it Snap, looks real. Where's the bullets go.

(*Beat*)

SNAP: In nah nah-er, clip but ain't no clip in it, look, here, it go here innah bottom, see diz hole innah handle?

SKEETER: Yeah, I see, we take it to school show Mistah Keith.

SNAP: Yeah, Mister Keef know what to do wid it. (*Takes it in his hand and pretends to shoot it.*) Kee-yow, kee-yow, get goin' Skeet, you always sayin' you be dah Flash. Outrun nah bullets. (*Pretends to shoot again.*) I'm Rambo Skeet, I'm Rambo wid a sheen-gun.

(*Beat*)

SKEETER: (*Takes off running down the alleyway.*) I'm nah Flash. Dah Flash can outrun lightning. Hah-hehaha.

SNAP: (*Points the gun at his life-long best friend and pretends to shoot.*) Packeyyou, keyyou, I think I got you Flash.

(*Beat*)

SKEETER: Nobody gets the Flash, not even Rambo wid a sheen gun. (*Skeeter smiles at Snap and sees him aim the gun again at him and takes off running.*)

SNAP: Key-yeow, pee-key-yow, chhhshhhpowkey-yeow. (*Looks down the sights just like his dad once showed him and sees his best friend. They had played in the same playpen together. He laughs and cocks the hammer then pulls the trigger, just like Rambo, and the lone bullet in the chamber hurls through the air and into his 92-pound best friend's back, slamming into his heart and killing him instantly.*)

END OF PLAY

Keith G. Laufenberg was a juvenile delinquent and joined the Marine Corps on his 17th birthday. He served three years and his novel "Semper-Fi-do-or-Die" was written 30 years later. He has been a professional boxer, carpenter, comedian, car salesman, Realtor, mortgage broker, bartender, bouncer, lifeguard, P.I. & Paralegal. He claims to use all these experiences, among others not so easily identified, in his writing(s). He has been writing articles, memoir, poetry, short stories and novels for over four decades and has hundreds of them published in Literary journals and magazines as well as online periodicals. He has one poetry chapbook, seven books of short stories. six novels, and one volume of collected plays, for sale in bookstores and e-stores worldwide. Visit his website @kglaufenberg.com

SONNY LISTON'S EYES & COLLECTED PLAYS

ISBN 13: 978-1-944699-04-8 (Play)
ISBN 13: 978-1-944699-05-5 (ebk)
PUBLISHED BY ROYAL CROWN ROYAL, LLC

Florida
Printed in the United States of America

Available in 2016 in all Bookstores and e-bookstores worldwide

LIBERTY CITY (A new Play)
KEITH G. LAUFENBERG

ISBN 13: 978-1-944699-02-4 (Play)
ISBN 13: 978-1-944699-03-1 (e-book)
PUBLISHED BY ROYAL CROWN ROYAL, LLC

Florida

Printed in the United States of America

Now available in 2016, in Bookstores and e-bookstores worldwide

I AM AN AMERICAN-A POETRY CHAPBOOK

KEITH G. LAUFENBERG

ISBN 13: 978-1-944699-00-0 (print)
ISBN 13: 978-1-944699-01-7 (ebk)
PUBLISHED BY ROYAL CROWN ROYAL, LLC

Florida
Printed in the United States of America

Royal Crown Royal Publishing

Available in 2016 at all bookstores and e-stores worldwide
Santa Claus, Satellites, Cellphones & Sinkholes & Collected Plays

KEITH G. LAUFENBERG

Collected Plays of Keith G. Laufenberg

Available soon in all bookstores & e-bookstores worldwide
PEACE ON EARTH & COLLECTED PLAYS

"THE ANGELS OF MONS."

KEITH G. LAUFENBERG

Available in bookstores & e-stores worldwide

BOOKS BY KEITH G. LAUFENBERG

NOVELS

MIAMI ROCK
SEMPER-FI-DO-OR-DIE
THE TOWER OF POWER
THE PROFIT FACTOR
SOUTH OF SOUTH BEACH
THE ANXIOUS ASSASSINS

SHORT STORY COLLECTIONS

MUHAMMAD'S REVENGE
STREETLIFE
BADMEDICINE
COWBOYS & INDIANS
THE MANLY ART
SAVING PRIMO
ANY OTHER NAME

POETRY CHAPBOOK

I AM AN AMERICAN

PLAYS

LIBERTY CITY-THE PLAY
SONNY LISTON'S EYES & COLLECTED PLAYS
PEACE ON EARTH & COLLECTED PLAYS
SANTA CLAUS, SATELLITES, CELLPHONES & SINKHOLES, IN SPRING HILL & COLLECTED PLAYS

Royal Crown Royal Publishing

Milton Keynes UK
Ingram Content Group UK Ltd.
UKHW011821041223
433765UK00002B/412